A place in Iggy Boy's hall of fame is an honor you could really live without . . .

It had to be some kind of horrible joke. His eyes began darting back and forth over the rows and rows of photographs neatly lining the walls. They showed people, people who at first were smiling—then not smiling—on their knees, pleading into the camera . . . then . . . unbelievable, grisly horror.

He saw Cameron Wheeler—hanging in the closet. And Spenguin, dead in the stairwell. And all the others. There were car accidents . . . and skiing accidents . . . and boating accidents . . . and suicides . . . and things he couldn't— and didn't care to—identify.

IN A
CROOKED
LITTLE HOUSE

IN A
CROOKED
LITTLE HOUSE

A.G. Cascone

WESTWIND®
Troll Associates

Printed in the United States of America.

10 9 8 7 6 5 4 3 2 1

To Tisha
for seeing us down that crooked mile

CHAPTER · 1

Iggy Boy hadn't wanted to shoot Mr. Spegman in the field house of Huntington Prep. Particularly not on the landing of a dimly lit cement stairwell. It was not at all what he had been hoping for, not at all what he had envisioned. In fact, it was totally inappropriate, totally meaningless, and totally disappointing.

He'd been hoping to shoot Mr. Spegman in Bowdin House, the most prestigious dormitory on campus, the dormitory that housed every blue-blooded, elitist little snot that Iggy Boy had ever known at Huntington Prep. It was the house that Spegman ran. The house to which Iggy Boy had been so thoughtlessly assigned. Where better to shoot the House Master than in his own house? Shooting Mr. Spegman there would have been so much more befitting—so much more inspiring—and there were so many colorful backdrops from which to choose.

Like the maintenance closet in the basement of

Bowdin House. That was definitely one of Iggy Boy's favorite places. It was where he'd shot Cameron Wheeler. The golden boy. Mr. Spegman's personal pet, his prize possession. The blond-haired, blue-eyed little wonder boy with the sixty-million-dollar trust fund and the entire staff of Huntington Prep in his daddy's back pocket. What a rush that had been — shooting Cameron Wheeler, all cramped up in that dirty little closet.

That was the first photograph Iggy Boy had ever taken. And it was perfect. Every detail in place. Truly a work of art. And Cameron Wheeler had been such an easy subject. Not like some of the others. Not like Mr. Spegman. No. Cornering Cameron had been a piece of cake. He was so self-absorbed. So easy to capture. And so photogenic. It was Iggy Boy's favorite shot, even now. Even after he had taken so many others, in so many meaningful locations, Cameron Wheeler's was still the best. That was the first time Iggy Boy had realized how much justice one little camera could wield. The first time he'd realized that he could capture all the old moments and preserve them forever.

Iggy Boy had so many memories he'd wanted to share with Mr. Spegman. And he had waited so many years to be able to shoot him . . . the right way. But now it was too late. Now it was all ruined. Now it was nothing but a big, fat letdown, all because Iggy Boy had lost his temper, all because Iggy Boy couldn't control his emotions. What a mistake. He should have learned by now. He'd ruined several of his most important pictures that way. And none had ever been more important to Iggy Boy than this.

After all, Iggy Boy owed everything he was to Mr. Spegman. No. This was not the way to pay homage to such a great man. Not here, not on the stairwell. There were no memories here—not important ones. Not for Iggy Boy—or for Mr. Spegman.

No. Their memories were in Bowdin House. In Mr. Spegman's private quarters, in Iggy Boy's room, in the hallways, and in the secret passageways, and the pantry, and the sitting room, and the basement. And the fourth-floor shower room.

Now *there* was a room with a view. A room full of memories. Shooting Mr. Spegman there would have been so much more fulfilling, so much more gratifying, so much more appropriate. What a shame. If only he had waited. If only he had been more patient. He might have been able to corner Mr. Spegman on the fourth floor, and beat the crap out of him, and drag him into the shower room, and tie him to the burning-hot pipes, and humiliate him in front of everyone in the dorm. They'd have just stood there and laughed at him and mocked him and spat at him. A real picture. A true Kodak moment.

Iggy Boy couldn't help feeling disgusted as he popped the flash on his camera. The sight of Mr. Spegman just lying there all sprawled out on the stairwell like an idiot was so unimpressive. Hardly worth the film. But Iggy Boy had no choice, not at this point. And even though he wanted to, he knew there was no way to drag Mr. Spegman over to Bowdin House for their final farewell. Not now, anyway. Not without being seen. The stairwell was just going to have to do.

"Okay, Mr. Spegman, sir," Iggy Boy looked through the lens, lining up the shot as best he could. "Smile for the yearbook."

Iggy Boy waited for a moment, as though he were expecting some sort of reaction. There was none.

"What's the matter with you, Spenguin? Didn't you hear me? I said smile for the yearbook, you fat slob!"

Iggy Boy kicked Mr. Spegman as hard as he could. He thought he heard a rib snap.

"You ignominious piece of scum," Iggy Boy took his first shot. "Did you think I would forget about you?" Iggy Boy reached down and grabbed Mr. Spegman by the hair, lifting his limp torso off the cement. "You better look at me when I address you, you ignoble little worm."

Iggy Boy let go of Mr. Spegman, allowing his dead body to fall back down on the landing. "Who looks like the half-wit now, huh, Mr. Spegman? Not Iggy Boy. No. Iggy Boy's gonna walk away from this clean. Just like he always does. But you're not going anywhere, are you, Spenguin? No. You're just gonna have to lie there and wait for somebody to find your pathetic little penguin corpse. And while some ignorant fool will inevitably throw you a pitiful little penguin funeral, no one will come. And you want to know why? Because everyone will be too busy having a party. A 'Spenguin's dead' party. It's just a shame that Iggy Boy can't take the credit he deserves. It's just going to be so annoying listening to people talk about how you 'accidentally' fell down three flights of stairs . . . how you 'accidentally' broke your neck. If only they knew. Iggy Boy would be a hero."

Iggy Boy shot the last picture on the roll. And as he heard the film rewind, he realized that he was using the special roll. The roll with all those pictures of Casey McCabe. And though he thought about reloading and getting a few more shots of Mr. Spegman, the idea of developing the film with Casey on it was much more exciting. She was the most beautiful girl Iggy Boy had ever known. A genuine masterpiece. So pure. So unaffected. So honest. It would be such a joy to spend the rest of the evening with her.

"See you in hell, Spenguin . . . sir."

With that, Iggy Boy left the field house just as he'd gotten in . . . totally unseen.

At least, that's what Iggy Boy believed.

CHAPTER · 2

By the time Casey McCabe walked into Mr. Spegman's second-period American Literature class, the party was already in full swing. Three days without Mr. Spegman, and the celebration continued. Not only was Mr. Spegman gone—a fact that appeared to be most gratifying to the majority of his students—but the administration had yet to find a replacement for him. And while all of Mr. Spegman's students had been directed to use his class time as a study period, no one bothered cracking a book. In fact, if it hadn't been for the fear of another faculty member popping in to take attendance or, worse yet, to take over the class, most of the students would not even have bothered to show up.

But since the idea of facing some sort of disciplinary action was less appealing than hanging out in Spegman's classoom for an hour, they'd decided to make the best of it. And the "best of it" meant using the time as a free period, a chance to socialize.

Casey hated second-period American Literature probably more than anyone else in the class. Not because she hated the subject. In fact, Casey was nearly the only student not actually assigned to the class; she'd taken it as an elective. She hated it because Mr. Spegman had done nothing but torment her from the very first day she'd stepped into the classroom. He'd assigned seats, making sure that Casey sat front row, center. Rumor had it that Mr. Spegman always put the scholarship students closest to his desk so that he could pick on those students and humiliate them more easily. And one thing Casey had learned in this class was that the rumor was true.

Four days out of five, Casey left Mr. Spegman's class and went straight to the bathroom to cry. She'd made a bargain with herself never to give him the satisfaction of breaking down in front of him. Even the time he'd photocopied her paper and passed it out to the class as an example of truly bad writing and even worse reasoning, she'd somehow managed to hold her head up until the bell had rung and she'd made it to the bathroom.

The paper wasn't that terrible. While it wasn't one of Casey's best, it didn't rate anything lower than a B. But to Mr. Spegman, B work from a scholarship student was practically a capital crime, particularly if that student was also a girl. Not only was Mr.

Spegman an insufferable snob, he was also a sexist snob. Though Huntington Prep had been coed for nearly ten years, Mr. Spegman refused to see the school as anything other than a bastion of male excellence.

Casey couldn't help feeling relieved that Mr. Spegman would no longer be teaching American Literature—or anything else, for that matter. Try as she might, Casey couldn't muster one good feeling about the man, or any genuine sorrow that he was gone. And while she wasn't thrilled with the idea of having to sit through another hour of "Spenguin" jokes and the latest Huntington Prep gossip, it sure beat having to face Mr. Spegman. As guilty as it made her feel, Casey McCabe had to admit that she was grateful that she would never have to see Mr. Spegman again.

As the bell rang, everyone in the room took a seat—an assigned seat, as if, even from the grave, Mr. Spegman retained some measure of power over them.

Casey took her seat—front row, center, right next to Chip Cimino. Chip was in the middle of yet another of his Mr. Spegman impersonations, to the amusement of Eddie Brewster.

"And furthermore, Mr. Brewster," Chip imitated Mr. Spegman's honking voice perfectly, "you are nothing but an ignorant little mooncalf with the attention span of an amoeba. Have I made myself clear?"

Eddie Brewster cracked up. "Mooncalf. Oh, man. And I still don't even know what it means."

"It means you're a moron," Chip laughed. As he turned back around in his seat, he noticed Casey.

"Well, well, well. If it isn't Miss McCabe." Again, he imitated Mr. Spegman. "So thoughtful of you to join us."

Casey had to smile in spite of herself. "You're starting to sound more like Mr. Spegman than Mr. Spegman."

"Is that so?"

Casey shook her head in amusement.

"So what do you think, are we home free again today?" Chip looked at his watch.

"I don't know."

"Maybe they forgot about us. Maybe if we all just sit here and keep our mouths shut, they'll forget this class even exists." Chip stretched out in his seat.

"Forget it, Chas. You're not that lucky." Casey laughed, not realizing her mistake.

Chip shot her a dirty look.

Casey realized what she'd said—realized what she'd called him. "Sorry," she shrugged apologetically.

She was never to refer to him as Chas, or even Chuckie for that matter. It wasn't appropriate — at least that was what he'd told her. He had an image to protect, an image that he'd spent years at Huntington Prep creating. An image that was held together by so many lies, Casey could barely keep track of them all. Fitting in at Huntington Prep was so important to Chip that he lied about everything. He lied about who he was and where he came from. He lied about his parents, and about all the money they didn't have. He lied about the summer home that didn't exist. And the vacations — he never took. And the car — he didn't own. He lied about his entire life, right down to his name. No one knew the truth except Casey. And no one ever questioned any of his lies. Except Mr. Spegman.

Casey could still remember how furious Chip had been with Mr. Spegman the day he informed the class that Chip was at the school on an athletic scholarship—a fact Chip had managed to keep quiet since his freshman year. It was right after Huntington Prep had lost its first football game of the season. And Mr. Spegman couldn't wait to get his digs into Chip. Chip was the captain of the team and Huntington Prep's star athlete. Word was that Chip was bound to make it all the way to the pros. Every college scout who visited the school was trying to recruit him. And Mr. Spegman knew it— and hated it. The loss of the game—even though it was only a scrimmage—gave Mr. Spegman enormous satisfaction, and all the ammunition he needed to get to Chip. He made some cruel joke about Chip being just another one of the "Athletic Department's academic charity cases whose athletic ability hardly warranted the benefits of an exclusive education." It was totally humiliating. And by the time lunch rolled around, everybody in the school was talking about Chip. About the scholarship.

Casey thought for sure that Chip would never talk his way out of it. But he did, and everyone believed him. Everyone believed that Chip had been planning to go to Lawrenceville Prep, or Exeter, or Choate. And that the only reason he'd ended up at Huntington was that they were so desperate to have him that they'd offered him a full scholarship as an incentive to come. And while he truly felt that Exeter was a much better choice, he'd opted for Huntington when his father offered to put the entire amount he was planning to spend on Chip's high school tuition into a trust account for Chip to use "on a rainy day." At a school where status was everything, Chip Cimino pretended to have it all.

"Isn't it nice to be rid of Spenguin," Chip mused.

"Don't call him that," Casey admonished. "Not now."

"Oh, like you never called him Spenguin," he shot back.

"Come on, Chip, he's dead."

"So what's that supposed to mean? That just

because the old coot trips and takes a header down the stairs, we're supposed to forget what a complete and total scumbag he was?"

"No, it's just that . . ." she trailed off, shaking her head in exasperation.

"Miss McCabe," Chip jumped back into his Spenguin routine. "May I remind you that you are in attendance at this school because of your supposed superior intellect. But you have yet to demonstrate to me the ability to learn or use language with even half the proficiency of Koko the gorilla." Chip saw that he'd hit the nerve he was looking for, and he dropped the imitation. "Remember what a big laugh that got?" He wasn't trying to hurt Casey, only to remind her how truly mean-spirited Mr. Spegman was, how undeserving of her sympathy. Chip would never do anything to hurt Casey. On the contrary, he would do almost anything to protect her.

"So what do you want me to say? That I'm happy that Mr. Spegman is dead?"

Chip shrugged. "Everyone else is."

"That's a terrible thing to say."

"No, it's not. It's the truth. And you want to know what the difference is between you and me, Casey? The difference is that I don't have a problem facing the truth."

Casey couldn't help but laugh at the irony of that

statement. "Is that so . . . Chuckie?" she whispered.

The irony was not lost on Chip, either. "I guess everybody in this place is a hypocrite in one way or another. Everybody but you." There was no sarcasm in his voice, only a tone of genuine admiration. But Chip was uncomfortable giving compliments, so he broke eye contact, rested his head against the back of the seat, closed his eyes, and prepared to nap through second-period American Literature for the third day in a row.

Chip's nap was quickly subverted by the appearance of Mr. Spegman's replacement.

Casey couldn't believe her eyes. She didn't dare hope that the teacher who had just walked into the classroom was going to take Spenguin's place.

"Good morning," he said as he closed the door behind him. "I am your new teacher. My name is Michael Gilliard."

As if every girl in class didn't already know that. Every girl at Huntington knew his name. When they'd spotted him on campus the first day of school, they'd all made a point of finding out who he was. He was new this year. He taught freshman English and coached J.V. soccer. He was twenty-seven years old. And, most importantly of all, he was not married. The only thing Casey could think was, "Wait until Margo finds out that I get to spend an hour every morning staring at this gorgeous man. She is definitely going to flip."

Margo Blake was Casey's best friend. Margo wasn't at all snobby, like most of the other kids at Huntington were. Her family had money, plenty of it. But only on her father's side. Her mother's family came from a neighborhood just like Casey's. They were just regular people. So Margo turned out to be just a regular person with a whole lot of money— and, now, a mad, raging, incurable crush on Mr. Gilliard, even though she had never spoken a word to him. Margo was just going to die when she found out about this.

Casey saw that Mr. Gilliard was smiling at her curiously. Then she realized that it was because she was smiling at him; well, not at *him*, exactly, but at the thought of telling Margo about him. Quickly she averted her gaze, praying that he wouldn't say anything to her.

"So what are we reading in this class?" He opened his briefcase on the desk.

No answer. Just some mumbling all around. Everybody, including Casey, was hoping that with a new teacher, they might also get a new book.

Mr. Gilliard checked the lesson plan. He laughed. "*Moby Dick*, huh?"

A collective groan went up from the class.

"It's not all that bad, is it?"

"It stinks," Chip answered.

"And your name is?"

"Chip Cimino."

"Well, Chip, I happen to think you're right. And so do a lot of other people. In fact, when the book was published, the reviews were almost all negative. So it seems that **you** are quite an astute reader." He was obviously kidding a little, but not in a mean way, not like Mr. Spegman.

"Yeah, I'm astute enough to tell you that this book's not worth finishing," Chip wisecracked.

The class voiced unanimous agreement.

"Well," Mr. Gilliard sighed, clearly still teasing, "I'm afraid that's where you're wrong. You see, good, bad, or indifferent, this book is still a classic. And in order to be well-read individuals, you absolutely must have some working knowledge of the classics."

"Not this one," Eddie Brewster shot back. "Couldn't we read something else?"

"Sorry, guys," Mr. Gilliard was serious. "It's not my call. I have to stick to the curriculum and try to make the best of it."

Another groan—the agony of defeat.

"I promise it's not going to be that bad." Reaching into his briefcase, he pulled out a hat shaped like a whale and put it on his head. "Call me Ishmael," he recited, throwing them the first line of *Moby Dick*. He pulled a string attached to the hat, and water sprayed out of the whale's blowhole.

The class laughed. Michael Gilliard was a hit.

From behind Casey a camera flash went off, followed by the whirring sound of film winding in a camera. She didn't have to turn around to know that it was Slater Laurence taking pictures again. He and his camera were the bane of everybody's existence these days.

Mr. Gilliard put his hands up, like a movie star trying to escape paparazzi. "Excuse me," he said to Slater. "What do you think you're doing?"

"Pictures for the yearbook," Slater answered unapologetically.

"Oh, no, no. Not in this class, pal. I do way too many stupid things to get and keep your attention, and I don't necessarily want to be preserved for posterity looking like an idiot. Okay?"

"Can I use this picture if it comes out?"

Mr. Gilliard thought about it for a minute. "Okay. But if I catch you taking another one, I get to make you eat the camera. Deal?"

"Don't worry about it," Slater answered, dropping the Nikon back into his backpack. "You won't catch me."

CHAPTER · 3

"Don't look now," Margo Blake whispered to Casey as they stood in line for lunch. "But I think Slater's taking pictures of you again."

Of course, the first thing Casey did was look. It wasn't hard to spot Slater because the lunchroom was still relatively empty. Margo and Casey always made a point of getting there early. If you weren't one of the first people to get to the salad bowl, all the good stuff was gone. Only the top layer was "tossed" to make it look good; underneath was only lettuce, and it wasn't always fresh. It was like everything else at Huntington; on the surface everything looked perfect, but underneath, you had to watch out.

Slater was sitting at a table by himself, his untouched tray of food in front of him. And he was indeed taking pictures of Casey again. When he saw her looking, he turned his camera very subtly to make it appear as though he were taking pictures of the kitchen staff. But Casey was not fooled.

Neither was Margo. "I'm telling you," she nudged Casey, "he's got a crush on you."

"*Sure* he does," Casey laughed it off. "He's got every girl in this school throwing herself at him, and he's pining away over me. I think you need a reality check, Margo."

"Oh, come on. I think the two of you would make a cute couple."

"Yeah, really cute." Casey was sarcastic. "The poorest kid in school dating the richest kid. Just think of the gossip *that* would start."

"I wish you wouldn't look at it that way."

"Why not? That's the way it is around here. And you know it. Besides," Casey decided to lighten up, "I think *you* and Slater are a much better match."

"Nah, I'm saving myself for Mr. Gilliard."

And so the conversation swung back to Mr. Gilliard again. Since Casey had told Margo about Mr. Gilliard's taking over Mr. Spegman's class, their conversation never seemed to stray far from the subject of Mr. Gilliard. "I can see it now," Casey joked, "I, Margo, take you, Mr. Gilliard, to be my lawfully wedded husband."

Margo laughed. "I definitely have to get on a first-name basis before *that*. But first I have to figure out how I'm going to be able to transfer into your class this late in the semester."

"You're not seriously thinking of changing classes just because of Mr. Gilliard."

"Why not?"

"I thought you loved your English class."

"What's not to love about moron English? All you've got to do to get an A is show up. Why else do you think ninety percent of the class signed up for it?" Margot rolled her eyes dramatically.

"You know how many people in Mr. Spegman's class tried to get into your class?"

"Well, now that it's not Spegman's class anymore, I'd gladly switch with any one of them."

Margo took her tray and headed straight for Slater's table. Casey followed, thinking maybe she should date Slater—just once, to shut Margo up.

There was only one problem with Slater Laurence: he was too, too rich. Half the dorms on campus, including Bowdin House, had been built with money donated to the school by one Laurence or another. Laurence money had also built the planetarium and the Laurence Arts Center, a theater worthy of Broadway. The Laurence family had been a presence at Huntington Prep since 1896 when the school was founded. You couldn't spit on that campus without hitting something that had "Laurence" written all over it. So it was very difficult to see Slater as just another student, when he was practically an institution. Even the teachers treated him differently.

It made Casey uncomfortable. The sad part was

that she knew that it made Slater uncomfortable, too. Casey assumed that that was why Slater kept to himself so much. All his interests—photography, writing, art, running, skiing—were individual pursuits. They were also a way of keeping people at a distance. In an ironic sort of way, Casey couldn't help feeling sorry for Slater.

Slater smiled as Margo slid into the seat across from him. "Hi, Margo," he said. And as Margo answered him, he turned his startling blue eyes on Casey. "Hi, Casey."

"How's it going, Slater?" She couldn't help feeling a little unnerved by his eyes. They were blue, like a husky dog's eyes. The icy color made them seem just a little cold and distant. There was no way to read them, no way to know what he was thinking as he sat there looking at her.

"So, Slater, want to trade English classes with me?" Margo broke the awkward moment.

"Not you, too," Slater moaned in mock dismay.

"I'm only human," Margo answered.

"Well, I'm human too. But I just can't see the attraction."

"That's because you don't have the right hormones," Margo joked.

"At the very least," Casey added her two cents to the conversation, "you have to admit he's a big improvement over Mr. Spegman."

"Does any girl in this school ever talk about anything else besides Mr. Gilliard anymore?" Trevor Caldwell had come up behind Casey without her noticing him. Chip was with him; so were Eddie Brewster and David Cross. They were the brat pack of Bowdin House.

"What's the matter, Trevor? Are you jealous?" Margo disliked Trevor immensely and never made any attempt to hide it.

Trevor leaned over Casey's chair, draping his arm around her shoulder. "I don't have anything to be jealous about. Do I, Casey?"

Chip elbowed Trevor the way he always did when he wanted Trevor to cut it out.

"That's right, Trevor. Why should you feel jealous of Mr. Gilliard just because he's older, smarter, and better-looking?" She wriggled out of his arm.

"Ouch," Eddie Brewster said.

"The Ice Princess strikes again," David Cross chimed in.

Trevor had been coming on to Casey since sophomore year. They'd even dated—once, and only once, a date Casey had later described to Margo as "four straight hours of octopus wrestling." Trevor did not know how to take "no" for an answer. Casey suspected it was because he'd rarely heard the word. He was the stereotypical spoiled rich kid who thought the world was his for the taking. And he couldn't seem to get it through his thick head that Casey was not interested.

In the beginning, she'd tried to let him down easy. She'd tried polite rejection and evasive action. Finally, she'd resorted to outright insults. All to no avail: Trevor would not leave her alone, would not keep his hands off her. He played it like it was a harmless game. And he always had Eddie and David egging him on like a pair of cheerleaders. But if it was a game, Casey did not enjoy it. And, clearly, neither did Chip.

"Well I know something that's going to make you girls extremely jealous," Trevor tried to bait them. "Guess who's taking over as House Master of Bowdin House?"

"Who?" Slater asked. He was interested. He lived in Bowdin House.

"Mr. Gilliard," Trevor answered smugly.

Neither Margo nor Casey would give him the satisfaction of a reaction.

"How do you know?" Slater pressed.

"I overheard the secretaries talking about it when I was in the office a little while ago."

"Don't you think it's strange that they would put a brand-new teacher in Bowdin House?" Eddie asked.

"It's probably only temporary," Trevor answered.

"You know who I think they should have given the job to?" Chip mused. "Flakey Jake."

All the Bowdin House boys, except Slater, laughed uproariously at that idea.

"Why not?" Trevor seconded the notion. "He's probably been here since the school was built."

"I guess it's about time for old Jake to get a promotion," Eddie joked.

"I think it's disgusting the way you always make fun of Jake." Casey defended Jake hotly.

"He's a maintenance man, Casey," Chip said, as though that were some sort of justification that Casey would understand. As though being a maintenance man made Jake less deserving of respect or even common decency. Chip, of all people, should have known better.

"You are a total jerk," Margo said, her voice dripping with disdain.

"Lighten up." David jumped into the conversation. "Jake doesn't even know we make fun of him."

"Jake doesn't even know he's alive half the time," Trevor continued. "In case you haven't noticed, the guy's got a serious drinking problem."

"He's got a problem even when he's sober," Eddie laughed. "I think all the booze has fried his brain beyond repair. All you've got to do is look at him to know nobody's home. I mean, you can be talking right to him and he stares at you like he doesn't hear a word you're saying."

"Or else he's talking to himself," David added.

"I'm telling you, sometimes he acts so crazy, he's scary."

"He's not scary," Casey protested. "And he's not crazy, either. Maybe if you tried to have a conversation with him instead of picking on him all the time, you'd find out what a nice man he really is."

Jake was always nice to Casey. He called her "Sunshine." Every time she ran into him, he gave her something—a piece of candy, or an apple, or a flower he'd picked. She always accepted his offerings graciously, and that made him smile. And while his behavior was undeniably strange at times, Casey didn't attribute it to his being crazy. Jake was sad and lonely, and certainly abused by the Bowdin House boys. But as far as Casey was concerned, Jake was just a sweet old man.

CHAPTER · 4

Jake couldn't open the maintenance closet in the basement of Bowdin House without thinking about Cameron Wheeler—without seeing him hanging there—dead. In the middle of the closet, the rope tied into a noose around his neck and wrapped around the pipes in the ceiling. It was the heavy rope, the rope Jake used to tie up all the garbage. It still made Jake chuckle to think of Cameron Wheeler, the biggest piece of trash in the school, hanging by the garbage rope.

Of course, Jake kept that joke to himself. He hadn't dared to tell anyone the truth about Cameron Wheeler. Not the police, not Spenguin, not the rest of the staff. And certainly not the boy's parents. Jake had just kept his mouth shut, like he always did. He'd just walked away from the whole thing, pretending to be as upset as everyone else. Yes, Jake had done one good job of making believe that Cameron Wheeler's death was a tragedy, just like they said it was.

But it was no tragedy at all. It was justice. And as far as Jake was concerned, death by hanging had probably been too good for Cameron. In the twenty-two years Jake had been employed at Huntington Prep as a "maintenance engineer," he had never met a boy he disliked more than Cameron Wheeler. And he had never been so happy to see someone go—until now.

Jake stepped into the maintenance closet and pulled the chain to turn on the light. He reached up to the second shelf, behind the tool box and under all the dust rags, and grabbed the bottle of Jack Daniels. He'd found it out in the bushes behind Bowdin House. That's where Jake always found the best liquor. After twenty-two years—more than half of them spent taking care of Bowdin House—Jake knew where all the good hiding spots were. All the secret places. And when it came to the good stuff, the really expensive stuff, Jake could always count on the boys in Bowdin House. Somebody was always hiding a bottle of something out in those bushes.

Jake opened the bottle and took a healthy swig. He reached into the pocket of his dirty, worn-out work pants and pulled out an eighteen-carat, diamond-encrusted black onyx ring. "Well, well, well," Jake looked over the ring. "What goes around, sure do come around. Now, ain't that right, Mr.

Spenguin?" Jake took another swig. "I mean, Mr. Spenguin . . . sir." Jake laughed as he slipped the ring onto his pinky finger to admire it.

It was Jake's ring. He'd found in June of 1985 in Bowdin House, in the sitting room under one of the sofa cushions. He'd turned it in to Mr. Spegman, just like he'd turned in all the other things he'd found in Bowdin House, except for the liquor. The liquor was fair game, and Jake needed a taste now and then. If he turned the liquor in, he'd only be stirring up trouble, anyway. Jake didn't want to stir up any trouble, not in that house. Personal belongings were different. Keeping something that rightfully belonged to someone else was stealing. And Jake was not a thief.

When he gave the ring to Mr. Spegman, Mr. Spegman had commended him for being so honest, for being such a "good worker." And then he'd promised Jake what he always promised Jake: "If nobody claims it, it's yours." But Jake had never gotten anything back from Mr. Spegman—except for the fancy pen he'd found in March of 1989 on the library floor. He'd only gotten *that* back because it didn't work. Anytime Jake found something that he was hoping would go unclaimed—like the camera he'd found in April of 1985, in the laundry room, or the Walkman he'd found in June of 1992, the one somebody had left behind in one of the dorm rooms over summer break—Mr. Spegman would tell him that the owner had come forward and that Jake couldn't have it back. That's what he'd told Jake about the ring, and Jake had believed him. Until December 17, 1986, when Mr. Spegman wore that very same ring to the faculty Christmas party.

Jake took the ring off his finger, wrapped it up in some dirty tissues he had in his back pocket, and put it in the bottom of the toolbox, right next to the Walkman. He took one last swig of the Jack Daniels before he carefully replaced the bottle under the dust rags on the second shelf. He grabbed the vacuum cleaner, turned out the light, closed the door to the closet, and headed back upstairs.

It was already half past two in the afternoon, and Jake had yet to start any of his usual chores. He'd spent the whole morning cleaning out Spegman's quarters. Now he was way behind his regular schedule and not at all happy with the idea that he still had eight to ten hours' worth of cleaning to do.

Bowdin House was immense. The sheer size of the place made it difficult for one person to keep up with. But that wasn't really the problem. In fact, as far as Jake was concerned, the house was manageable. The problem was, the Bowdin House boys were not. If it weren't for the forty-six filthy, rotten, do-nothing, no-good, slimy little worms running around tearing up the place full-time, keeping up with Bowdin House would have been a whole heck of a lot easier for Jake. And now, with classes almost over for the day, all the slimy little worms would start slithering in, and Jake wouldn't be able to get a thing done in peace. Yeah, thanks to Spenguin, Jake was sure that midnight would be rolling around long before he got to sit his aching behind down. Even dead, Spenguin managed to provide Jake with plenty of aggravation.

Jake had just started vacuuming the main sitting room when Chip, Trevor, Eddie, and David came in and plopped themselves down on the sofas, making sure to stretch their legs out far enough to get in Jake's way.

"Hey, Jake. How's it hanging?" David asked loudly.

Jake paid no attention.

"What's the matter with you, Dave?" Trevor got up and stood directly in front of Jake. "You know he can't hear you." Trevor got right up in Jake's face and pretended to talk in sign language, making all kinds of rude gestures as he screamed at the top of his lungs. "Dave said . . . hey, Jake . . . how's it hanging?"

Jake just nodded. Just like he always did. Eddie and David cracked up.

"Man, Flakey Jake's been hitting the bottle early today." Trevor waved his hand in front of his face like he was trying to clear the air.

Eddie unwrapped a piece of candy and threw the wrapper on the floor, directly in front of Jake. "Hey, Jake, you missed something."

Jake bent down and picked up the wrapper as though it had been lying there the whole time. He was as good at pretending not to see as he was at pretending not to hear. Jake learned a lot about people that way.

"Watch this," Trevor said as he walked over to the outlet that the vacuum was plugged into. "This is the best." Trevor pulled the plug.

Jake continued to vacuum while the boys cracked up. This was too funny.

Just then Slater walked into the room and saw what was going on. He'd seen this scene way too many times. Not once had he found it amusing.

"What's the matter with you guys?" Slater walked over to the outlet and plugged the vacuum back in. "Can't you find something better to do with your time?"

Jake just kept on vacuuming.

"You know, Slater, you're really lucky you've got money, 'cause I've gotta tell you, your personality really sucks." Trevor started out of the room. "I'm going over to the field house to watch the cheerleaders get changed for practice. Anybody want to come?"

Eddie and David jumped up like a shot. "I'm in," they said in unison.

"What about you, Chipster, you coming?" Trevor asked.

"Yeah. I'll walk over there with you. I'm gonna work out anyway."

The four of them headed out.

Jake shut off the vacuum and turned to Slater. "Ignorant. That's what those boys are. Just plain ignorant. If it weren't for you, Sammy, this whole house would be full of garbage. Yes, sir. But you're a good boy, Sammy. A real good boy. And don't you think for one minute that old Jake don't know that."

"It's Slater, Jake." Slater corrected him for the eighteen-bazillionth time.

"I know that too, Sammy," Jake assured him as he patted him on the back.

Slater smiled. Jake had never once called him by his right name in all the years he'd been at Huntington Prep. And Slater was sure that even if he showed Jake his birth certificate and wore a name badge full-time, Jake would still insist on calling him Sammy.

"It's gonna be interesting to see what kind of trouble those boys get into once the new House Master moves in. Real interesting."

"When is Mr. Gilliard moving in, Jake?"

"Next weekend. At least, that's what they tell me."

"Is he going to be living in Spenguin's quarters?"

"No. He's gonna be up on the fourth floor. That's why they're up there fixin' the place, doin' all that construction."

"I thought they were just going to renovate the fourth floor. You know, make it nicer," Slater said. "For the seniors."

"Yeah, well, that's what they said they were gonna do last year when they moved all the seniors down to the third floor with the junior slugs. But now they've changed their minds. Now they're gonna give the whole floor to Mr. Gilliard. Except for the library, I think. If you ask me, Sammy, it's a mistake. I mean, how can he keep an eye on things if he's gonna live way up there on the fourth floor? Know what I mean?"

Slater nodded. "What about Mr. Spegman's quarters?"

"Oh, you ain't gonna believe this, Sammy. They're gonna rip down all the walls in that apartment and turn the whole thing into a sittin' room. A sittin' room with a kitchen." Jake shook his head in disgust. "Like I need to be cleanin' up another sitting room in this house. Like four big sittin' rooms on three different floors ain't enough. Now they want to go and put another one down here. Like anybody in their right mind would wanna be sittin' in there anyway." Jake started winding up the vacuum cord. "This ain't a good day for me, Sammy, and it ain't gonna be over until tomorrow at this rate. You know why, Sammy?" Jake didn't wait for Slater to respond before he continued rambling. "'Cause old Jake had to spend all day cleanin' out the new sittin' room, packin' up all Spenguin's belongings, so that his fat penguin of a sister can come pick them up. Tell you what, Sammy, that woman is meaner than he was, if you can believe that. Ugly, too. Has to be the ugliest woman this side of hell."

Slater laughed.

"That's why I'm so far behind today. And there ain't getting nothing done with those ignoramuses around."

"You shouldn't let them treat you like that, Jake." Slater meant it. "You shouldn't let them get away with it."

"Don't you worry yourself about it, Sammy. Old Jake can take care of himself." He patted Slater on the back again. "Besides, Sammy, what goes around sure do come around. You remember that."

CHAPTER · 5

Iggy Boy was in his secret place, watching the workmen finish up for the day on the fourth floor. So many changes were being made in order to accommodate Mr. Gilliard. So many memories were being destroyed. Now there would be no more dorm rooms on the fourth floor. There would be no more shower room. Only the library would remain. The library—and Iggy Boy's secret place.

Iggy Boy didn't want Mr. Gilliard on the fourth floor. It added too many complications. Too many variables. And it was way too close for Iggy Boy to feel comfortable. He wanted Mr. Gilliard to live in Spenguin's quarters, where he belonged. It's what Iggy Boy had planned. Now it was ruined. Now, everything would be different. And all because of Mr. Gilliard.

Iggy Boy hated Mr. Gilliard. He hated the way he looked, hated the way he acted, hated the way the girls walked around thinking he was something special. If they only knew the truth. If they only knew what Iggy Boy knew. They'd know that Mr. Gilliard was nothing more than a sham . . . a joke . . . a total disappointment. And as far as Iggy Boy was concerned, Mr. Gilliard did not belong at Huntington Prep . . . and he certainly did not belong in Bowdin House.

But there was only so much that Iggy Boy could do. Only so much that Iggy Boy could control. So Iggy Boy was just going to have to deal with the situation. He was just going to have to make the best of it—at least for a little while.

Iggy Boy walked around his secret place looking at all the memories. All the moments he'd preserved. He pinned up the picture of Mr. Gilliard, the only one he had. And as Iggy Boy looked at it, he couldn't help snickering at how stupid Mr. Gilliard looked, at how humiliating the shot really was. Yeah. It was definitely a yearbook picture. And he'd pinned it up right next to the shot of Mr. Spegman lying in the stairwell. How appropriate. The new, living House Master hanging right next to the old, dead one.

Iggy Boy liked to admire his work. In fact, there were days Iggy Boy would spend hours just looking at all the pictures, hours reliving all the magic moments. He couldn't help staring at the picture of Spenguin. It was actually pretty good. Not what he'd originally hoped for, not what it was supposed to be, but good nonetheless. He could even see the spit on Spenguin's face. No doubt about it, Iggy Boy had talent.

The shot of Spenguin was supposed to be his last, the grand finale, the final tribute to his glory days at Huntington Prep. But Iggy Boy was beginning to feel differently. Yeah, Iggy Boy was beginning to realize that there was still a lot of cleaning up that needed to be done in Bowdin House. A lot of garbage that still needed to be put out.

Then there was Casey. Casey McCabe. Iggy Boy devoted an entire wall of his secret place to Casey McCabe. She was so special. So beautiful. So pure. There was no way Iggy Boy was going to let any of the filth of Bowdin House get anywhere near her, no way he was going to let the only innocence he'd ever known at Huntington Prep be tarnished. No. Iggy Boy would protect her. And Iggy Boy would stay with her . . . forever.

CHAPTER · 6

Casey crossed the footbridge onto the island, unaware that she was being watched. The little island in the middle of the artificial lake was Casey's own personal refuge. It was the only place at Huntington that afforded her any sense of privacy, the only place she felt she wasn't being watched.

Even in the dead of winter Casey would go out to the island to study or read or just sit and think. She enjoyed the solitude. More than that, she needed the time alone to keep herself focused, to put things into perspective. At Huntington Prep keeping things in perspective was no small task, especially if you happened to be from the wrong side of the tracks.

Huntington was fiercely competitive, both academically and socially. The truth was that Casey felt she just didn't belong there. Her senior year wasn't shaping up to be any more comfortable than her freshman year.

It wasn't that Casey couldn't cut it academically. Academically, Casey could compete and excel and appear to do it effortlessly. She was regularly ranked near the top of her class, a standing she actually worked long and hard to maintain. But Casey didn't mind hard work. She rather enjoyed it. It was why she was there, after all.

Her social life at Huntington was another matter entirely. Margo was her only close friend. And while she had plenty of male attention, it was perfectly clear to her that she was the kind of girl that Huntington boys wanted to date but not the kind of girl that any of them would ever consider bringing home. Casey was an outsider, a girl from the wrong side of the tracks. She felt as out of place as a JCPenney model in a J. Crew catalogue. For a long time Casey had tried to affect the perfect preppie look of rumpled comfort. But there was no way to make permanent press slacks look like expensive cotton chinos, or knock-off loafers look like the hundred- dollar originals. So Casey had stopped trying and found her own style.

Instead of wrinkled and fashionably mismatched, Casey chose to be pressed, tucked-in, and coordinated. When she was voted "best dressed" by the yearbook committee, Casey couldn't help wondering whether it was a compliment or a joke. Whatever their intention, she felt a twinge of discomfort at being set apart.

Sometimes Casey thought it would be easier to be

a misfit or an outcast. The misfits and outcasts tended to form groups of their own, so even they had the sense of belonging that Casey so sorely missed.

Probably the only other person at Huntington capable of understanding how Casey felt was Slater Laurence. In fact, Casey suspected that he felt exactly the same way, only for different reasons. She wished she had the courage to ask him about it, to ask him if he felt as lonely and out of place as she did. Sometimes she allowed herself to believe that Margo was right, that she and Slater would make a good couple, that they were somehow kindred spirits.

But thinking of Slater as an outsider seemed quite ridiculous to Casey as she sat down on the "Laurence Bench" and set her books beside her. The bench was a memorial to yet another Laurence, a Martin Laurence, who'd graduated from Huntington in 1936 and been killed in World War II. He was Slater's granduncle, his grandfather's brother. And it was Slater's grandfather who'd had the marble bench put on the island and who'd planted the beautiful maple tree that shaded it, in memory of his brother.

Casey wondered if any of the Laurences had ever taken the time to appreciate this place. She wondered if they knew how beautiful and peaceful it was. To her, this memorial was more touching and more impressive than any of the other monuments bearing the Laurence name. As she sat there, taking it all in, as she had a thousand times before, she found herself thinking about Slater again and wondering if he ever spent time on the island.

CHAPTER · 7

He was watching her from the woods across the lake, the woods that blanketed the far end of Huntington's property, secluding the campus from the outside world. The woods were dense and deep and not easily accessible. Iggy Boy knew every inch of them like the back of his hand. He'd spent plenty of time in the woods, particularly on the night he'd buried Justin Taylor. What a colossal pain in the neck that had been. It was the first and last time Iggy Boy had ever taken it on himself to dispose of a body. It was way too much work . . . and totally unnecessary. But that was ancient history. And while Iggy Boy couldn't help but be somewhat amused by the idea that he was practically standing on the grave of his "missing school chum," his thoughts were only momentarily diverted from *her* . . . Casey McCabe.

He watched her take off her coat and lay it neatly beside her on the bench as he snapped the zoom lens onto his Nikon. And as Casey stretched out, obviously enjoying the unseasonably warm weather, Iggy Boy snapped the first picture on the roll, and the second, and the third . . .

Iggy Boy photographed every little move Casey made. He wanted so much to be able to capture everything he possibly could about her. And everything she did, every move she made, was so appealing.

Iggy Boy had taken hundreds of pictures of Casey on the island. He had pictures of Casey reading, pictures of Casey writing, pictures of Casey just daydreaming. Those were his favorites—the pictures of Casey just daydreaming. He had devoted one entire wall to those pictures. Late at night, when everyone else was asleep, Iggy Boy would lose himself in the pictures of Casey McCabe, imagining himself to be the object of all her thoughts, and needs, and desires. Just the mere idea of being with Casey was more exciting to Iggy Boy than anything he had ever done, than anything else he had ever imagined.

He watched Casey pick up one of the books beside her and open it to where the bookmark was. It was *Moby Dick*. And Iggy Boy could practically see what page she was on. Through the zoom lens, Casey looked close enough to touch. And Iggy Boy couldn't help reaching out into thin air and pretending that he was running his fingers through

Casey's beautiful light-brown hair. In his mind's eye, she laid her head on his shoulder, feeling safe and warm and desired.

Iggy Boy wanted to be near Casey more than anything else in the whole world—even more than he had wanted to do justice to Spenguin and all the others. It was almost unnerving. It had been a very long time since Iggy Boy had last had feelings like this. And feelings like this were always difficult for Iggy Boy to control.

In fact, as Iggy Boy snapped the last picture on the roll, he thought about putting the camera away . . . and leaving the woods . . . and going over to the island . . . so that he could really be close to Casey, close enough so that he could really touch her . . . so that she could really lay her head on his shoulder . . . and he could really run his fingers through her beautiful, light-brown hair.

CHAPTER · 8

Casey never saw him coming, never heard a sound. So when she finished the chapter and glanced up and saw him standing right in front of her, looking down at her, she screamed involuntarily. He just kept standing there, smiling.

"How long have you been here?" she asked coolly.

"Not long, baby, not long."

"You shouldn't sneak up on people like that." Her tone turned icy.

"I didn't sneak up on you. You were so into that book, a bomb could have gone off and you wouldn't have noticed."

Casey shrugged it off dismissively. She had nothing to say to him, and she hoped he'd take the hint and leave. But he didn't. And more uncomfortable than his presence was the fact that he didn't even try to make polite conversation.

"What do you want?" Casey asked bluntly.

"Now that's a loaded question," he leered.

"What are you doing here?" She spoke very

slowly, making her meaning, she hoped, crystal clear.

"I was just passing by and saw you sitting out here all by yourself. And you looked so lonely. I mean, nobody should be alone on 'Fantasy Island.'"

Casey rolled her eyes in disgust. "Fantasy Island." She knew that was what the jocks called the island. She knew it was a favorite make-out spot after dark. And, if the gossip she'd heard was correct, there were other late-night activities on that island of which Casey wanted no part.

"Look, Trevor, I appreciate your concern," she said sarcastically. "But I am not lonely. I have five chapters to read for tomorrow. And I came out here so that I could be alone, so that I wouldn't be interrupted." She buried her face in the book, determined to make him go away.

But Trevor was equally determined to stay. "Looks like you really love that book."

"No. Actually, I hate it," she answered without looking up.

"You and everybody else in Gilliard's class."

Casey heard the disdain in Trevor's voice when he said Mr. Gilliard's name, and she was amused by it. Mr. Gilliard was not terribly popular with a lot of the guys. Casey was sure it was because they were so painfully jealous of him.

"Let me ask you something," Trevor persisted in

his efforts to get her attention. "What makes Mr. Gilliard such hot stuff?"

Casey just laughed. She wasn't about to dignify the question with a response. Besides, she was afraid that to engage in a defense of Mr. Gilliard would make obvious the embarrassing truth that she had as big a crush on him as every other girl at the school. She'd tried to be sophisticated about it, tried to convince herself that it was silly to let herself give in to romantic notions about a teacher. But she couldn't help it. The more she saw of Mr. Gilliard, the more convinced she was that he was totally perfect in every way. Michael Gilliard looked good, he smelled good, and Casey had even let herself imagine that having his arms around her would feel good. *And* he had a great personality. It was impossible *not* to have a crush on him.

"Whaddaya mean?" Trevor responded to her silence. "Don't tell me you're in love with him, too?"

"No," Casey lied, a little self-consciously. "But you sure are jealous of him, aren't you?"

"Jealous of *him*? You've gotta be kidding. The guy's a total jerk. You should see him when he gets into House Master mode, he makes Spenguin look like a really nice guy."

"Mr. Spegman probably *was* a nice guy before he moved into Bowdin House. I wouldn't be House Master of that zoo without a whip and a chair.

Frankly, I feel sorry for Mr. Gilliard."

"Listen, I didn't come all the way out here to talk to you about Mr. Gilliard."

"Then what were you doing? Following me?"

"Would it get me brownie points if I said yes?"

Casey blew it off.

Trevor pushed her books aside and sat down next to her. "How would you like to go into town to see a movie with me on Friday night?"

Trevor was clearly trying to be charming. For Trevor, that meant he'd asked the question without being lewd or offensive. So Casey decided to respond as politely as she could. "No, thank you."

"Saturday night, then," Trevor pushed.

"I don't think so."

"When?" Trevor wanted an answer. An affirmative answer. A specific date.

"Trevor, please, we've been through this before. You and I just aren't very compatible. Can't we just leave it at that?"

"No. We're not gonna just leave it at that."

Something in the tone of his voice bothered her. She felt somehow threatened. And for a split second, she felt the urge to get up and run away. But she immediately dismissed that feeling as being way out of proportion.

"I really like you, Casey." He sounded sincere and even a little vulnerable. "And if you gave yourself half a chance, I know that you would like me, too."

And before she could say anything, he moved toward her to kiss her. She dodged it, just barely, and slid off the bench onto her feet.

Undaunted, Trevor was beside her again in no time, with his arms around her, trying to kiss her again. She twisted her head away from him. "Trevor, stop it," she demanded. And when it was clear to her that he had no intention of stopping, she managed to free her arm and she slapped him.

His hand went to his face in surprise. But surprise quickly gave way to utter, terrifying rage. "You stupid little tramp," he spat.

Casey couldn't believe what she was seeing. Even as his fist made contact with her face, even as she fell over backward and her head hit the ground, she couldn't believe it. And she was almost frozen with panic as she realized that he was still coming at her. Almost. But something inside Casey refused to be a victim. As Trevor lowered his body over hers, she kneed him in the groin as hard as she could. It was what her father had told her to do if anything like this ever happened to her. And he'd warned her to deliver the blow with full force and without hesitation in order to incapacitate her attacker, not just make him angrier. She'd done it correctly. Trevor fell over next to her, immobilized with pain.

In her entire life Casey had never been forced to

fight, not physically. Of course, like everyone, she wondered how she would respond were she ever challenged. And now she knew. She'd defended herself, successfully.

She scrambled to her feet, as Trevor continued to writhe in pain. "Don't you ever touch me again!" she warned him. Then she snatched up her books and her coat and fled.

CHAPTER • 9

Iggy Boy couldn't stop the screaming in his head. Rage was bubbling through his veins like a volcano ready to erupt. He was losing control, and he was beginning to feel as though he was going to lose his mind.

He had to calm down. He had to direct his thoughts. It was taking every ounce of strength Iggy Boy had to stop himself from running out of the woods and swimming across the lake . . . to the island . . . to Trevor Caldwell . . . so that he could tear his flesh apart with his bare hands . . . and rip his organs out one by one . . . and hold them up in front of Trevor's face . . . so that Trevor could identify each and every one of them while he lay there begging Iggy Boy for forgiveness . . . begging Iggy Boy for salvation.

But there would be no salvation for Trevor Caldwell. No salvation, and no redemption. Only justice. Iggy Boy had to think. He had to give proper consideration to the matter. He had to weigh it carefully. He had to handle it appropriately. While acting on impulse always provided momentary pleasure, it was always a mistake. And there were just too many variables.

Iggy Boy gathered his thoughts as he snapped yet another picture of Trevor Caldwell, a truly touching shot of Trevor tucking himself in, looking around to make sure that no one had seen what went on.

And no one had, no one but Iggy Boy. Not only had he seen it, Iggy Boy had managed to capture every moment of it, frame by frame. It was preserved forever. So there would be no way for Trevor Caldwell to deny what went on. No way at all. Because Iggy Boy had taken frame after frame of Trevor touching her, frame after frame of Trevor hurting her, frame after frame of Trevor humiliating her.

And wouldn't Trevor be surprised. Wouldn't he just die when Iggy Boy showed him all the shots he had. That was definitely going to be the fun part—for Trevor, anyway. Iggy Boy's enjoyment would come *after* he showed Trevor the pictures, after Trevor got on his knees and begged Iggy Boy for forgiveness, like the ignominious piece of scum that he was. After Trevor found himself sobbing like a baby while Iggy Boy touched him and hurt him and humiliated him. If only he could share it all with Casey so that she would know that justice was being served.

Casey. Poor, sweet, innocent, beautiful Casey. How

could this have happened? How could he have allowed this to happen? He should have seen it coming. He should have expected it. After all, Trevor was a Bowdin House boy. And Iggy Boy was all too well aware of the kind of filth that was bred in Bowdin House. Even with Spenguin dead, it seemed that the evil Bowdin House continued to flourish. And he had no one to blame. No one but himself— and Mr. Gilliard.

Why hadn't Mr. Gilliard done anything about the boys in Bowdin House? After all, he was the House Master now. It was up to him to run the house properly, not Iggy Boy. Iggy Boy had tried to give Mr. Gilliard a chance, but Mr. Gilliard had failed him. It was becoming painfully clear to Iggy Boy that sooner or later Mr. Gilliard would have to go. Not because he was like Spenguin. No. Mr. Gilliard wasn't at all like Spenguin. At least Spenguin had determination and total self-confidence, as misguided as he was. Mr. Gilliard was just a wimp. A waste. A nothing. Just like Iggy Boy had known he'd turn out to be.

As Iggy Boy saw Trevor leaving the island, his thoughts turned immediately back to Casey. He had to get out of the woods. He had to make sure she was all right.

One thing was certain. No one would ever get near Casey McCabe again. No one would ever be allowed to touch her again. No one but Iggy Boy.

CHAPTER · 10

Casey half-walked, half-ran the quarter of a mile back to her dorm. She took the back way, using a path that was seldom traveled. All she wanted was to be able to make it back to her own room unseen.

She kept her head down, moving as quickly and purposefully as she could, fighting every minute to maintain her composure. She concentrated on the sound of her own heavy breathing, using it as a rhythm to put one foot in front of the other, propelling her closer to safety.

It wasn't until her dorm was in sight that Casey began to fall apart. Not far to go, but now every step was a struggle. She picked up her pace and a few choked sobs escaped from her throat. Her adrenaline had stopped pumping, and what she really wanted to do was just lie down in the grass and cry. Casey wiped at her nose with the back of her hand and it came away bloody. There was blood down the front of her sweater as well. She couldn't let anyone see her like this. She had to get to her room, and fast. So Casey summoned one final burst of energy and sprinted toward Kimberly Hall, the massive, Georgian-style building that provided housing for all the senior girls.

As Casey came off the grass and onto the path, not fifty yards from the front door of her building, she ran head-on into Mr. Gilliard. He let out a startled gasp and Casey lost her balance in the collision. But Mr. Gilliard dropped his briefcase and reached out to steady her and kept her from falling.

"I'm sorry," Casey tried to say in a normal tone of voice, but it came out as a sob. She also tried to hide her face from him.

But it was too late. Mr. Gilliard took a step back, still holding onto her shoulders. "Casey, what happened to you?" His voice was calm, authoritative, yet full of concern.

Not only was Casey incapable of coming up with a good lie, she also doubted her ability to talk without bursting into tears. "Nothing," she managed to choke out.

"Come with me," he said gently, propelling her with one hand on her shoulder.

"Where?" Casey stiffened.

"Just over there." He pointed a little way down the path. "Let's go sit on that bench so we can talk privately for a few minutes."

He led her along silently, each of them trying to

formulate what to say. When they got to the bench Casey sat down. Mr. Gilliard sat beside her and rested his elbows on his knees, folding his hands in front of him. "Casey, please tell me what happened to you."

"Nothing," she insisted. "Really."

"Nothing," he repeated incredulously. "Sweetheart, the side of your face is swollen and turning a lovely shade of green and purple. Your nose is bleeding. And your lip is split. Now, *something* happened. And I want you to tell me what it was."

"I fell," she lied badly, too ashamed to tell him the truth. "I can be so clumsy sometimes. I tripped and I fell." She couldn't tell whether he was buying it or not. "It's really very embarrassing," she attempted a smile. "Anyway, I'd really like to get inside and get cleaned up before anybody else sees how stupid I am."

"I don't think so," he said gently.

"Excuse me?"

"I'm sorry, Casey. I just can't let this go. You didn't fall. At least, not without some help. What I'm looking at here—impossible as it seems—is the result of a fist fight. I know that because I've been involved in enough of them myself to know what the results look like. What has me confused is that I would never have figured you for the type who would duke it out with somebody." He was trying to be cute, trying to go easy, trying to get her to open up to him.

But the truth was too awful, at least to Casey. She didn't want anybody to know what had happened to her. She could just imagine the gossip this would cause. Not that Mr. Gilliard would tell anyone. But things had a way of getting around. It was best just to keep the story to herself. After all, she had taken care of the situation. She just wanted it to be over. She wanted to forget about what had happened.

"Casey, who hit you?" He took the direct approach.

She shook her head.

"You know the punishment for one student striking another is suspension."

"Please, Mr. Gilliard, can't we just drop it?"

"I'm afraid not. Not with the way you look."

She said nothing.

"Casey, why are you protecting this person?"

"I'm not protecting him," she blurted out. "I'm protecting myself."

"How is that?"

Casey saw an opening to get out of this conversation. "Because I could be suspended, too."

"For what reason?"

"Because I landed the first blow."

"I see." He nodded thoughtfully, patiently. "Let me ask you something. Does the other guy look worse than you do?"

"Not really." Her nose started bleeding again and she wiped at it.

Mr. Gilliard took a clean white handkerchief out of his pocket and handed it to her. "One more question," he continued. "What made you hit another student?"

They were back on shaky ground. "I don't know," she shrugged.

"You mean to tell me that you just walked up to another student, made a fist, and punched him?"

Evasive action. "I didn't punch him, I slapped him."

"Ah. Now we're getting somewhere. Another student—a male student—did something that provoked you to slap him. The only question that remains is, what did he do?" He waited for an explanation from Casey but when none was forthcoming, he went on. "Well, it's pretty banal, but one particular reason springs to mind."

"Yes," Casey conceded. "That was the reason."

"Unwelcome advances," he clarified it.

She nodded, grateful that he had phrased it so politely.

"In my book, that's an acceptable reason."

Casey heard footsteps approaching and looked up to see Slater running on the path, headed right toward them. He was dressed in Athletic Department shorts and a T-shirt and was dripping with sweat. Casey turned her head away, waiting for him to pass by.

Instead, he stopped right in front of her. "My God, Casey, what happened to you?"

"It's all right, Slater," Mr. Gilliard assured him. It was also a hint for Slater to move along. But the hint must have been too subtle.

"What happened to her?" he demanded of Mr. Gilliard.

"It's okay," Mr. Gilliard repeated. Then he purposefully changed the subject. "Where have you been running today?" He pointed toward Slater's muddy running shoes.

"Same course I do every day," he answered absently, his eyes focused on Casey.

"Well, you'd better finish it out, or your muscles are going to seize up." A more direct hint.

Slater hesitated.

"It's under control, Slater," Mr. Gilliard told him.

"Are you sure you're okay?" Slater asked Casey directly.

She nodded. "Yeah. I just took a bad fall, that's all. But I'm okay. Thanks."

He knew it was a lie, but there was nothing left for Slater to do but be on his way.

Casey watched as Slater headed down the path. Then she stood up. "I really want to get inside. I don't want anybody else to see me."

"Just a minute, Casey." Mr. Gilliard stood facing her. "I want to know who did this to you."

"Why?"

"Because I can't allow something like this to go unpunished."

"Mr. Gilliard, please," Casey begged. "Please don't do this to me. Don't you understand? The whole thing would just be a circus. He'll only get a slap on the wrist anyway. And I'll end up looking like a fool." She put her head down and began to cry.

Mr. Gilliard took her by the shoulders again. "Casey, you were wronged. You are the wronged party. And as such, you are entitled—obligated, even—to seek justice for what happened to you. Young women simply cannot allow young men to get away with this kind of behavior."

"He didn't get away with it. I took care of myself. I got away. Please don't make this a public issue. It's tough enough around here without my asking for more trouble." Her eyes met his and held them. His soft, brown eyes were full of tenderness and compassion and, at that moment, conflict. "Please," she whispered again.

It was Mr. Gilliard who broke eye contact. He relented. "All right. Against my better judgment, I won't report this."

She heaved a sigh of relief. "Thank you."

"There is one condition. I want his name. Because

if anything like this ever happens again—to you or anyone else—I will personally see to it that he is expelled from this school. You tell me who did this, and I will keep it to myself so long as he continues to behave like a gentleman."

She hesitated. It seemed like forever before she could bring herself to say his name out loud. "Trevor Caldwell."

Mr. Gilliard shook his head in disgust. For a second Casey was afraid he would renege on his promise. Then he took her hand and patted it comfortingly. "Okay," he said. "Okay. We'll just put this away. And I hope we'll never have to talk about it again. Unless you want to, unless you need to talk to someone."

She put her free hand over his. "Thank you, Mr. Gilliard."

"You go ahead inside and get cleaned up now."

And as she headed toward the dorm, Casey felt sure that she'd done the right thing by telling Mr. Gilliard. She looked back over her shoulder and saw him standing there watching her, waiting for her to get safely inside. He smiled encouragingly. But Casey couldn't help feeling a twinge of guilt at the thought that Mr. Gilliard was not at all sure he'd done the right thing by promising to keep her secret.

CHAPTER • 11

"Davey, Davey, Davey. Check out the body on that babe," Eddie Brewster practically drooled. "Come on, zoom in on her, will ya?"

"No way, no way, she didn't get surgery to look like that," David Cross said, as he used the television remote to comply with Eddie's wishes. The television in the sitting room of Bowdin House, as well as the stereo and video equipment, was state of the art. On top of all the usual amenities, the 47-inch set was capable of multichannel viewing—in three languages—as well as auto playback, freeze frame, and zoom focusing—a feature that Eddie and David had been using quite a lot in the past few minutes. They had come across the "Page Six" girls on one of the afternoon talk shows, and all of them were wearing bikinis.

"Please don't tell me you guys are watching another skin flick," Chip said as he came into the room and plopped himself down on the sofa. "What do you want to do, throw Mr. Gilliard into another fit?"

"No, thank you. I swear there's something really wrong with that guy," David said, scanning the rest of the girls sitting on the panel.

"For real," Eddie agreed. "I mean, what kind of a guy gets bent about skin flicks?"

"Yeah, right," David added. "I'm telling you the guy is sick or something. Besides, he's not even here yet. And there's no way he can say anything about us watching a talk show. Every one knows that talk shows are educational and informative . . ."

Chip laughed. "Yeah, well, if it's a talk show, how come you guys have the sound turned down?"

"'Cause it's a lot more fun just looking at them," David shot back. "Who needs to hear a bunch of bimbettes talking?"

"Come on, turn it up," Chip said as he leaned back into the cushions. "It looks like the audience is getting pretty hostile."

"Yeah, they're all screaming about how girls in bikinis don't belong on page six of a newspaper. And I think they're right. They ought to be on the cover." Eddie laughed as he continued leering at the screen.

Trevor came into the room and sat down in one of the high-back chairs without saying a word. He popped open the can of soda he was holding and took a swig.

"Hey, Trev," Eddie and David said simultaneously.

Trevor barely nodded back.

Chip didn't bother to acknowledge Trevor at all.

"Boy, you're in a real charming mood," David said sarcastically.

"You got a problem with that?" Trevor shot back, ready for a fight. Picking on David and Eddie was actually one of Trevor's favorite pastimes, particularly when he needed to vent some frustration. They were both such easy targets. And there was nothing that Trevor liked better than a "no-challenge" kind of challenge.

"Did I say I had a problem with that?" David wanted to diffuse the situation for no reason other than that the "Page Six" girls were still on the TV. "I don't have a problem with that." David immediately turned his attention back to the screen.

Trevor let it go.

"Wouldn't it be great if we had a 'Page Six' girl in the school paper?" Eddie was truly excited by the idea. "Somebody ought to suggest it. I bet there'd be a lot of girls who'd want to do it."

"Great idea," Chip said sarcastically. "Aside from the fact that we don't even have a page six in the school paper, I'm sure it would go over real big with the administration."

"I think it's a great idea." Trevor was almost hostile in his tone. "At least then we could start weeding out all the little teasers around here . . . like your sweet little friend Casey McCabe. One of these days, somebody's gonna give that girl just what she's asking for."

Chip had to stop himself from belting Trevor in the mouth. Trevor had no right to talk about Casey that way. Casey had never done a thing to provoke Trevor's constant harassment, his constant come-ons. And she certainly didn't deserve his disrespect. But Chip had to play it cool. After all, Trevor was his best friend—at least for appearances sake. So Chip tried to affect a tone of indifference. "I don't understand why she gets to you so much. She's not all that great-looking anyway." Chip practically choked on the lie.

"What happened, Trev? The Ice Princess shoot you down again?" David wanted to know.

"Let me tell you something, Dave. The Ice Princess just melted all over me," Trevor shot back. "And I'll tell you what. As far as I'm concerned, that girl is nothing more than poor white trash."

Chip could already feel the blood pulsating in his brain. And he knew that it was going to take every ounce of strength he had to sit there, composed, listening to Trevor spew what he was sure would be lies.

"What happened?" Eddie finally gave Trevor his full attention, now that the talk show was over.

"I'm walking down by the lake, coming back from the field house," Trevor proceeded to spew. "When Casey runs up behind me and puts her hands over my eyes . . . you know, like all the girls do, that stupid game they play when they're trying to be cute . . . you know what I'm talking about?"

Eddie and David both nodded in recognition, while Chip braced himself for the rest of the story.

"So I'm standing there, with Casey practically hanging on my back, thinking to myself 'No way, Casey's coming on to me,' right? And the next thing you know we're walking down by the lake together, and she's goofing around, and we're talking about all kinds of stupid stuff, okay? Then she starts telling me how she's been doing a lot of thinking about me lately, and how she really wanted to go out with me sophomore year." Trevor took another swig of his soda. "You guys remember? She was always throwing herself at me back then."

"I thought she only went out with you once sophomore year. And didn't she tell you she hated your guts?" David was as tactful as David got.

"No," Trevor snapped back. "She didn't tell me she hated my guts, but she *did* break it off. And get this. She tells me that the only reason she broke it off was because all the other girls hated her for going out with me—they were all jealous and crap. And she just couldn't take it."

Chip was beginning to feel sick to his stomach.

"Anyway," Trevor continued, "here's the best part. I ask her if she wants to walk over to 'Fantasy Island.'

And, get this, she says yes. We all know what that means, right? So we're sitting there on the bench, and I ask her if she wants to go out Friday night— to, like, a movie or something. And she practically jumps out of her skin, she's so excited. And by now, I'm getting pretty excited myself, know what I mean?"

David and Eddie were getting pretty excited just listening.

"So I lean over and kiss her. And then, with like no warning at all, she snaps out on me. I'm telling you, I couldn't believe it. It was like she was out of her mind or something. You had to see it. She was hittin' me, and punchin' me, kickin' the crap out of me. I swear, I had to deck her just to get her off of me. And then, when I tell her to drop dead and that I want nothing to do with her, she starts crying. Can you believe this? And she starts tellin' me how much she still likes me, how much she wants to be with me, and how sorry she is that she acted that way, and can we still go out on Friday night." Trevor shook his head in amazement. "I'll tell you what, Chipster, somebody better tell that little wacko how lucky she is that I'm such a nice guy. If she's smart, she'll stay as far away from me as possible, 'cause I don't need the aggravation." With that, Trevor got up and headed for the stairs.

CHAPTER · 12

Through one of the air ducts in the basement of Bowdin House, Jake had been listening to the entire conversation taking place in the sitting room upstairs. He knew where every pipe and every wire and every duct in that basement led. He'd had years to figure it all out. After all, Jake was the "maintenance engineer"—a job he was extremely proud of, a job he took very seriously. So Jake made sure he knew about all the workings in Bowdin House, all the goings on. It was the only way to run the house properly. And that was very important to Jake.

"That boy's gonna be awfully sorry when his behind ends up just like Cameron Wheeler's." Jake shook his head in disgust. "One of these days these boys are gonna learn that what goes around sure do come around—especially in this house." Jake belted down the last of the whiskey he had. The last taste, and it was hardly enough to steady his nerves. He'd been hitting the booze a lot lately and he knew it. In fact, Jake hadn't needed to drink like this since the year Sammy had gotten into all that trouble. Bad trouble. Only Jake couldn't remember exactly what it was.

Ever since the Spenguin episode, Jake had been having a hard time keeping his mind straight. Even sleeping well was becoming a problem again. Jake had been having a lot of bad dreams. Half the time, he wasn't sure they were dreams at all. Half the time, he was almost sure they were really happening. And the only thing that seemed to help clear his head up was the liquor.

Jake opened up the door to the maintenance closet and started digging through his old gym bag, looking for his emergency stash. The gym bag wasn't really his. He'd found it in the trash can in the boys' locker room in March of 1989. And neither was his emergency stash. That belonged to Trevor Caldwell. Jake had watched him hide an entire case of the stuff out on "Fantasy Island" not three weeks earlier. It was Absolut vodka. And Jake found the taste of vodka almost as repulsive as he found the mere sight of Trevor Caldwell. But until Jake could find some time to clean out the bushes behind Bowdin House, Trevor Caldwell's vodka was just going to have to do.

Jake always got a kick out of the fact that the Bowdin House boys thought that "Fantasy Island" was their private little playground. He couldn't believe that they were all ignorant enough to believe that nobody could possibly see the goings on out there without crossing the bridge. And the biggest ignoramus of them all was Trevor Caldwell. What'd he think was happening to the liquor he was hiding out there? Field mice? Jake had to laugh. "What a stupid, stupid boy. Don't you know that Jake sees everything—everywhere." Jake forced down a swallow of the vodka. "There are no secret places."

There were no more voices coming through the air duct that led up to the sitting room. Just quiet. Even the television had been shut off. Jake was pretty sure that the room had been cleared out. And he was grateful. He didn't want to run into any one of those boys. Not now. Not the way he was feeling. Not with a belly full of whiskey and a shot of vodka. He just wouldn't be able to trust himself. No. There would be no way he could be responsible for his actions should one of those boys be stupid enough to say the wrong thing, stupid enough even to try and talk about little Sunshine like that in front of Jake. No sir. One thing was certain: now was definitely not the time to be messin' with old Jake.

When Jake went upstairs, he found he was right. The sitting room was empty. And Jake always liked to take the opportunity, when the room was clear, to watch some TV on the big screen himself. To Jake it was almost like sitting in a movie theater. And

Spenguin had told him it was okay for him to watch the big TV as long as his chores were finished for the day, and as long as he wasn't getting in anybody's way. And the new House Master hadn't said a word about it. So Jake turned on the TV, hoping to find a good rerun of one of his favorite shows. He needed to stay calm for awhile, and watching the TV always seemed to help him relax a bit.

"Hey, Jake." Slater passed through the sitting room and headed for the stairs. He barely looked at Jake.

"Hey, Sammy, where you going so fast?" Jake was genuinely fond of Slater—always liked seeing him. In fact, Slater was the only boy in Bowdin House Jake didn't want to see go.

"Nowhere, Jake. I'm just going upstairs to change." Slater started up the stairs.

Jake knew something was wrong because Slater had barely said hello. It was like he didn't want to be bothered, and that was never the way he was, not with Jake, anyway. He'd at least spend a few minutes talking with Jake—sometimes even sit around and watch the TV with him. "Something wrong, Sammy?" Jake was really concerned.

"No, Jake. Nothing's wrong," Slater lied. "I just want to change."

"Boy," Jake shook his head at the sight of Slater's filthy clothes. "How do you get so dirty?"

"Running, Jake." Slater took another step up the stairs.

"Where at? Last time I looked, there were no mud pits on this campus."

Slater smiled. "Everywhere, Jake. You know that. I run everywhere."

"Yeah, well if I was you, Sammy, I'd run my behind into my room and stay there. 'Cause you don't even want to know the latest piece of trash making its way around this house." Jake was sure that would get Slater's attention. It always did. All Jake had to do was let on one little bit to Slater that something bad had happened—that he was upset about anything at all—and Slater was always willing to listen.

Slater came back down the stairs, just like Jake knew he would. "What happened, Jake? Did somebody do something to you?"

Jake laughed. "Sammy, how many times I got to tell you, old Jake can take care of himself. It's that little girl I'm worried about."

"What little girl, Jake?" Slater knew immediately that Jake was talking about Casey, even before Jake answered. "Casey?"

Jake nodded. "Yeah, that's the one."

"Why are you worried about Casey, Jake?"

"Because that Trevor boy has been runnin' around this house tellin' tall tales about that sweet little girl.

I'm tellin' you, Sammy, that boy is trouble. With a capital *T*. You know it, and I know it. He's got all the other ignorant worms in this house believing she chased after him, that he almost had his way with her. But that ain't the truth, Sammy. You know it as well as I do. It just ain't the truth. You couldn't get that boy to tell the truth if his life depended on it."

"I just saw Casey, Jake. She was with Mr. Gilliard. Her face was all messed up, like she'd been in a fight or something. But she told me she just fell down."

"Yeah, she fell down, Sammy. She fell down 'cause that boy hit her. And now he's walking around this house claiming self-defense. Self-defense! Can you imagine that? That boy's so ignorant he can't even make up a good story. I sure do hope that Mr. Gilliard knows how to handle this situation, 'cause I sure wouldn't want to to see anything bad happen. No sir. Jake ain't in no mood for that. You just watch out for that girl, you hear me, Sammy?"

"Sure, Jake. I'll watch out for her."

"You're a good boy, Sammy," Jake said as he patted Slater on the back. "A real good boy."

Chapter · 13

Chip couldn't look at Casey's face without flinching. He sat in second-period American Literature, not hearing a word that Mr. Gilliard was saying. All Chip could think about was Casey sitting there beside him and how he hadn't been able to protect her after all.

It had been three days since the incident out on the island. Every day that passed, every day that Chip had to look at Casey's beautiful face so bruised and discolored, he became more determined to find a way to make Trevor pay for it.

"I had to deck her just to get her off me," Trevor had said. It was a lie. Chip knew it was a lie. But being a liar was the least of Trevor's character flaws.

Chip hated Trevor. He always had. But up until now, Chip had managed to tolerate him, more than tolerate him. Trevor was convinced that Chip was his best friend. And that was because up until now, Trevor had been useful to Chip.

Trevor had arrived at Huntington Prep in

sophomore year. At that point he had already been thrown out of every other exclusive prep school on the East Coast. The only thing that had gotten Trevor into Huntington was the huge donation his father made to the school. And the only thing that kept Trevor there was the fact that his father matched the donation year after year.

No question about it; money was everything at Huntington. If you didn't have money, lots of money, you were nobody, nothing. Unless, like Chip, you managed to latch onto a perfect patsy, like Trevor. Trevor loved to throw his father's money around, and he was particularly generous with his best friend. Most of the things Chip owned—and all of the nicest things—were charged to Trevor's father's American Express card.

The state-of-the-art CD player, the fancy pen, the status watch —Chip owed it all to Trevor. Chip wore expensive chinos and expensive loafers. He even had a couple of custom-made jackets from the best men's shop in town. Thanks to Trevor, Chip had money. Chip was somebody. And it had felt good. Until now.

Trevor had crossed the line. Over the past few days Chip had found himself slipping deeper and deeper into a murderous rage. He wanted to make Trevor pay, but he wasn't about to act rashly. He had to think it out carefully. He wanted to come up with something that would really be fun, something that would appeal to his sense of poetic justice. How about that; he really had learned something in English class. Poetic justice: a punishment ironically suited to the crime, the ultimate what-goes-around-comes-around. It would come to him. He just had to be patient. Good ideas never came on command. They always came in the shower or at three o'clock in the morning when everyone else was asleep.

Chip put thoughts of Trevor aside and decided he'd better tune into whatever it was that Mr. Gilliard was saying. He was half-way through his now-that-we've-finished-the-book-it's-time-to-write-a-paper spiel.

"I want you to choose a character from the book and write your paper as though you were that character. A word of warning; should you choose to be Moby Dick, you had better be particularly insightful or delightfully funny. I am counting on the fact that we have exhausted the supply of Moby Dick jokes here in the classroom. However, if you feel the overwhelming urge to include a new one in your paper, it had better make me fall off my chair with laughter. In order to help you out a little, I have put together a sheet of helpful hints, thought-provoking questions, and even possible opening sentences. Feel free to use anything that works for you."

Mr. Gilliard passed out copies of the paper. Chip

noticed how Mr. Gilliard paused in front of Casey's desk, how he looked at her face. Chip wondered if Mr. Gilliard believed the line Casey was giving to anybody who asked what happened to her. "I'm so clumsy. I tripped and fell." Was Gilliard that stupid? Didn't he hear things around Bowdin House? Any House Master with half a brain should have been able to put two and two together and come up with Trevor Caldwell.

In Chip's opinion Michael Gilliard was a complete and total waste. If he couldn't figure out what was going on in his own house, right under his nose, he didn't deserve to be in Bowdin House. And if he did know—or even suspect—and chose to ignore it, he didn't deserve to live. Even Spenguin—who, Chip was sure, was rotting in Hell—would have done something about this situation.

The bell rang and Chip grabbed his things, anxious to get out of there. If he had to sit there and look at Gilliard's pretty boy face for one more second, he didn't think he'd be able to resist the urge to deck him.

"This paper is going to be a nightmare," Casey said as she stepped out into the hallway behind Chip.

"You're telling me," he muttered back. But he did not turn around to look at her, because he was already too angry to bear the sight of her face.

CHAPTER · 14

By the time Parents' Day rolled around, the bruise on Casey's face was almost completely gone. And the slight discoloration that was left was easily covered with makeup. Nobody would have guessed that there had ever been an injury. Nobody except Casey's father.

Jack McCabe wasn't out of the car two minutes when he figured out that something had happened to his daughter's face. The tip-off was the makeup. Casey never wore any. So his curiosity prompted closer examination. And, with what Casey was sure must have been X-ray vision, he spotted the last vestiges of the bruise she'd tried so hard to conceal from him.

"So how'd you get the shiner?" he asked.

"It was an accident," Casey answered. She put her arm through her father's and led him down the path toward the football field where the day's festivities were about to begin with "the big game."

"I should hope it was an accident," her father

laughed. "You don't come to a school like this to learn how to fight."

There was a part of Casey that wished she could tell her father that she *had* gotten the black eye in a fight. He would have been proud of her; not that she fought, but that she fought back. And it probably would have comforted him to know that she could. But then she would have to tell him the circumstances of the fight.

She didn't even want to think about how her father might react, what he might do to Trevor. It had been hard enough to control Margo after she'd pried the truth out of Casey. But Margo understood Casey's reasons for wanting to keep it quiet, and she'd promised not to confront Trevor, although she did practically hiss every time she saw him. But there would be no controlling her father.

"So what happened?"

"I was playing field hockey." She'd thought out her story in advance, just in case he noticed. She knew he would never believe the story she told everyone else. "I got hit in the face by a wild swing."

"Maybe you shouldn't play field hockey anymore." He was serious.

"Daddy, it was a freak accident."

"Why didn't you tell me about it when it happened?"

"Because it wasn't worth mentioning. It looked

much worse than it was. And I didn't want you to worry."

"I *do* worry about you. All the time."

Casey knew that was true. Jack McCabe was a worrier. He'd suffered too many losses in his life not to be. Both his parents had died when he was still young, in his twenties, when Casey was just a baby. His brother was killed in a car accident a few years later. And then, came the worst blow of all. He had lost his wife, Casey's mother, to cancer when Casey was only seven years old. Casey couldn't imagine how her father had found the strength to go on. But somehow he did. He'd managed to raise Casey alone. Even though it was just the two of them, and even though she still desperately missed her mother, Casey felt that she had a stronger sense of family than many of the "privileged" kids at Huntington.

Casey's father was not a wealthy man. He was an electrician, and he had worked long and hard for everything he had. And everything he had, he invested in Casey. He wanted his daughter to enjoy all the advantages in life that he hadn't had. Still, when Casey was offered the scholarship to Huntington, both she and her father agonized over the decision. Casey didn't want to leave home, and her father was afraid to let her go. But in the end, he convinced her—and himself—that it was the opportunity of a lifetime. And so, as much to fulfill his dreams as her own, Casey had accepted the invitation to Huntington and worked hard to make the most of it.

Casey saw the delight on her father's face as they walked along together, saw his eyes drinking in the beauty of the place. He was thrilled to have his daughter here, living in these surroundings, just like the child of a millionaire. Because she knew this, Casey didn't have the heart to let on to him that life at Huntington was ever anything less than ideal.

Of course, Parents' Day was specifically designed to portray life at Huntington as ideal, right down to a guaranteed win in football. They were always scheduled to play their weakest rival on Parents' Day. This year was no exception, and Huntington walked away with a trampling victory.

As the players were leaving the field, Chip spotted Casey and her father and made his way over to them.

"Great game," Jack McCabe congratulated Chip, patting him on the back.

"Not much of a fight." Chip was being humble and honest, not cocky.

"I'm afraid not," Jack laughed. "Still, it's always exciting to see you play, Chuckie."

"Thanks."

Casey saw Chip look around uncomfortably to make sure no one was listening. She was grateful that he was subtle about it. She was sure her father hadn't noticed. Jack McCabe had no idea that Chip lied about his background, and Casey figured it was best for all of them just to keep it that way.

"I couldn't be more proud of you if you were my own kid."

"Well, I may be able to play some ball, but it's your kid whose got all the brains," Chip turned the focus of attention to Casey. "And the looks, too."

Jack McCabe glowed with pride. "Yes, she does."

Chip noticed his coach beckoning. "I've got to go," he excused himself. "I'll catch you later."

"I'm glad to see that he's doing so well here," Casey's father said once Chip was out of earshot. "It's a miracle when a kid like that makes it, with all the obstacles he's had in his life."

Casey nodded sympathetically. She was the only person at Huntington who knew what Chip's home life was like. And she'd agreed to keep it a secret because it was so terrible. His father was abusive, his mother alcoholic. It was a wonder that Chip could function at all, a wonder that he wasn't some kind of psycho. He certainly had every excuse to be.

"Yeah, that poor kid's had a hard way to go." He looked at his own daughter. "I guess you both have," he said sadly.

"No, Daddy. Not me. I have more than I'm entitled to. Because I have you."

Jack McCabe threw his arms around his daughter and held her tight.

CHAPTER · 15

"Don't you ever quit?" Adam Laurence asked, amused by the fact that Slater was still taking pictures.

"No. I don't," Slater answered as he turned the camera on his brother, feeling somewhat embarrassed. He'd been taking pictures of Casey and her father as they walked up to Huntington Hall. And while he knew that Adam had no idea what he was shooting, he couldn't help but feel like he'd been caught in the act. "I never quit," Slater said as he snapped a picture of his brother. "If I quit, how would we ever have gotten the famous 'Adam in the flippers' picture?"

Adam laughed. "You know Dad still has that picture on his desk."

"Get out." Slater laughed too.

"I'm serious. And every time I'm in his office for a meeting or something—you know, with other people—Dad always makes sure to point it out. Then, for the next half hour, I have to sit there while everyone else in the room tries to top Dad by humiliating their own children with one crazy story after the next. Which isn't so bad, really, except that, no matter what, I always seem to win the 'stupid kid tricks' competition hands down. 'Cause thanks to you, Dad's the only guy in the room with a visual aid."

Slater cracked up. The flipper picture was definitely funny. In fact, it was one of Slater's favorite shots of his brother. The picture had been taken at Adam's graduation party, when Slater was only seven years old. To this day Adam couldn't quite explain what it was that had possessed him to dive off the diving board with the flippers on his hands, except to say that it had seemed like a funny idea at the time. But the joke was on Adam. He had emerged from the pool looking an awful lot like the title character of *Creature from the Black Lagoon*. The pressure of the dive had forced the flippers all the way up Adam's arms so that the heels were up near his shoulders, and the openings for the toes were wrapped securely around his forearms—so securely that their father had had to cut them off.

For Adam, it was one of those embarrassing little episodes that people prefer to forget. But Adam couldn't forget because Slater had documented the entire episode with his camera. Even as a child, there had been no denying his talent.

"Wanna skip the lunch and go for a swim?" Slater teased Adam, barely able to keep a straight face.

"Very funny," Adam tried to hide his own amusement.

"No, I'm serious. I'll take a picture of you with the flippers on your feet this time. I promise." Slater snapped another picture of his brother. "And we can give it to Dad." He took another shot. "Come on, think of how proud he'll be."

Adam cracked up. "You'd better get that camera away from me, pal." Adam started waving his hands in front of Slater's face in a mock attempt at slapping him. Slater playfully dodged his advances. "Haven't you done enough emotional damage to me with that thing?"

"Not a chance." And with that, Slater and his brother started roughhousing, just as they used to do when Slater was a kid.

Adam was Slater's only brother, and he was almost eleven years older than Slater. By the time Slater was out of diapers, Adam was already a freshman at Huntington Prep. But while Slater pretty much grew up as an only child—with Adam at Huntington and then Brown before Slater was even past eighth grade—he and Adam had somehow managed to stay close. Adam had always made time for Slater, even when Slater was little. And Slater was grateful that he did. He loved his brother as much as he admired and respected him. Beyond a doubt, Adam was one of the nicest people Slater knew. Slater was sure that even if he weren't Adam's brother, he'd still feel the same way.

Having Adam at Huntington for the day felt really

good. In fact, Slater couldn't help wishing that he and Adam were much closer in age so that they could have attended Huntington together. Adam was probably the only person on earth who could understand just how difficult Slater's life at Huntington really was. Because Adam had lived through it himself.

As if all the usual insecurities that just came with being a teenager weren't enough, the Laurence name made fitting in at Huntington incredibly difficult. It made any kind of anonymity completely impossible. No matter what, Slater couldn't help feeling that any attention he got had a whole lot more to do with his last name than with who he really was.

"What do you say we break this thing up before we start attracting a crowd, huh?" Adam gave his brother one last shot in the arm. "Besides, I'm starving to death."

When Slater and his brother reached the lawn in front of Huntington Hall, they headed straight for the food tent. As they made their way through the buffet line, Slater couldn't help noticing Casey and her father sitting at one of the tables. He fought the urge to reach for his camera. And he tried desperately not to stare.

He'd already taken at least thirty pictures of Casey that day, mostly at the game, where he was supposed to be photographing the plays from the sidelines. But for two of the pictures, ones he'd taken before the game, Casey had actually posed. One was with her father. And Slater couldn't help being touched by the look of genuine admiration Casey had on her face as she looked directly up at her father and not into the camera. Slater wondered if Casey's father knew how lucky he was to have Casey look at him that way—love him that way.

Slater was sure that Casey's father was a wonderful man even though he had only met Mr. McCabe once or twice. Even then, it had been just briefly, just long enough to say hello, really. But he'd raised Casey. As far as Slater was concerned, if her father was half of what she was, he was definitely a great man. He was sure that the picture he'd taken had captured the two of them beautifully.

But that wasn't the picture Slater was dying to develop. No, the picture he couldn't wait to see was the one he had taken of Casey all by herself, the one her father had insisted he take, assuring Slater that it would probably be the prettiest picture in the yearbook. Casey had blushed. And Slater had wanted so badly to tell her father that he didn't need any assurances of that, that every picture he had of Casey was beautiful, that if it were up to Slater, the entire yearbook would be devoted to pictures of her. But he didn't. He couldn't. And he felt his own face turning red as he took the shot of Casey, standing just two feet away, looking directly at him, smiling that beautiful smile. It was the first time Slater had taken a picture of her that close.

"She's definitely the prettiest girl I've seen all day." Adam could hardly have missed noticing that Slater hadn't taken his eyes off Casey.

Adam's remark startled Slater and brought him immediately back down to earth. "Who?" Slater tried to finesse it.

Adam smiled. "You know who. You've been staring at her all day. If I had to lay money on it, I'd say that you probably took more pictures of her today than you did of the game."

"You're crazy," Slater lied, knowing full well that his brother could see right through him.

"Hey, do they still have the big Mischief Night dance at Bowdin?"

"Yeah," Slater said tentatively, wondering where Adam was heading with the question. "Why?"

"Why don't you ask her to be your date? She seems like a nice girl. And I bet she'd say yes."

Slater rolled his eyes at his brother just like a little kid who heard something really stupid.

"You've got nothing to lose. If I had never asked Beth to that dance, she might have ended up marrying somebody else." Adam paused to make sure he had Slater's undivided attention. "And you might never have gotten the chance to be an uncle." Adam threw out the news he had been waiting to tell Slater all day.

Slater's heart stopped. He was truly hoping that he'd heard correctly. "Excuse me?"

"Looks like you're gonna be an uncle." Adam could barely control the excitement in his voice. "We just found out that Beth is pregnant."

"I can't believe it," Slater said as he hugged his brother. "I can't believe you're gonna be a dad." Slater was thrilled. "Do Mom and Dad know yet?"

"Are you kidding me? Beth called them the minute we left the doctor's office. Dad's so excited, he's planning to cut the business trip short so that he and Mom can get back here right away. I told him not to hurry, that the baby wouldn't be here for another seven or eight months. But Dad wants us all to go out and celebrate. And Mom is already agonizing over whether she wants the baby to call her 'grandmom,' or 'mom-mom,' or 'nana.'"

Slater laughed. And for the next half hour, over lunch, Slater and Adam couldn't stop talking about the family and the baby and how good it was to be together.

After lunch Slater and Adam made their way out to the back lawn, where all the activities were.

"Adam Laurence. I'll be a son-of-a-gun."

Slater and Adam turned around to see Jake standing by the wine table.

"Well, if it isn't Jake." Adam was genuinely happy to see him and headed right over. Slater followed. "Jake," Adam said as he extended his hand. "It's really good to see you."

Jake took Adam's hand and shook it enthusiastically. "Adam Laurence. Will you look at you."

"Geez, I can't believe you remember me." Adam meant it.

"Are you kidding me? I never forget a face. Do I, Sammy?"

Slater's jaw practically fell onto his chest and he had to fight the urge to burst out laughing. "No, Jake. You never do." Slater looked at his brother, who was equally amused.

"So what've you been doing with yourself these days, Adam? Last Sammy tells me, you were running the big foundation."

"Yeah, I still am, Jake."

"I read it in the paper all the time, how the family's always donating money to one good cause or another. Sure does make me proud. But how come they never mention your name? I always look for it." Jake thought that somehow this was an injustice.

"Oh, I don't know, Jake," Adam laughed. "I guess it's because I don't want them to."

"Let me get you a glass of wine." Jake didn't bother waiting for the bartender. He poured the wine himself and handed it to Adam. "I'd get you some too, Sammy, but we'd be askin' for a whole lot of trouble."

"That's okay, Jake. I don't want any." Slater meant it. He didn't really like to drink. It always made him feel too out of control.

"Thanks, Jake." As Adam took a sip, Slater couldn't help seeing Adam looking around guiltily.

"It's okay, Adam," Slater laughed. "You're a grown-up now, remember?"

Adam laughed at himself. "It's just so weird to be on this campus with a legal drink in my hand. I still feel like I'm seventeen, you know? The thought of disciplinary action around this place still scares me."

"Oh, come on. No way it was as bad back then as it is now," Slater commented.

"Are you kidding me?" Adam retorted. "When I was here, Spenguin was in his prime. And let me tell you something, that man could move like greased lightning."

"Not anymore." Jake downed the wine he'd been sipping. "Ain't that right, Sammy?"

"Sure is, Jake," Slater answered, trying to keep a straight face.

"Oh, geez. That was really terrible of me, wasn't it? Going off about Mr. Spegman like that. Believe it or not, I really was sorry to hear about the accident."

"No need to be apologizing to me," Jake shook his head. "Ain't no crying around here over that man's dyin'. And between you and me and that lamppost over there, Spenguin's death wasn't no accident. Ain't that right, Sammy?"

Slater looked a bit startled and immediately turned around to make sure that nobody had overheard.

What a thing to say. But Slater's relief at knowing the conversation was private gave way to concern over what he should say in response. Luckily, Jake just continued.

"What goes around sure do come around. You know that. Both you boys know that." Jake rubbed his head as though he were responding to the shooting pain of an extremely bad headache. His hands were trembling. His entire face flushed and then just as suddenly paled..

"Are you okay, Jake?" Adam reacted to the startling change in Jake's demeanor.

For a moment Jake didn't respond, at least not to Adam. He just stood there mumbling to himself incoherently.

"Jake, are you okay?" Adam repeated as he reached out to touch Jake's shoulder.

"Oh, yeah," Jake answered finally, trying to pull himself together. "I'm fine. Must be the wine or somethin'. Maybe I better walk around a bit. You know, walk it off, clear my head."

"Are you sure you're all right, Jake?" Slater was genuinely concerned.

"How many times I got to tell you, Sammy, that old Jake can take care of himself. Always worrying about me, this boy," Jake smiled at Adam. "He's a good boy, your brother. A real good boy." He patted Slater on the back just like he always did when he said that. "Now, don't you go leaving here, Adam Laurence, without saying good-bye to old Jake."

"I won't," Adam assured him.

As Jake walked away, Slater caught sight of Mr. Gilliard. He pointed him out to Adam as Bowdin's new House Master. Then, just when Slater had convinced Adam there was no point in introducing him, Mr. Gilliard started walking toward them.

"How're ya doin', Mr. Gilliard," Slater said as he approached. Slater knew that Mr. Gilliard hadn't walked over to talk to him, that he was only coming over to get a drink. Still Slater felt uneasy, still he had to force a smile. Ever since the Trevor-Casey incident —an incident that Mr. Gilliard failed to handle appropriately—Slater had hardly been able to stand to look at the man. As far as Slater was concerned, Mr. Gilliard's "nice guy" image was nothing more than a facade. Nice guys didn't turn the other cheek when innocent people got hurt. No matter what.

"Hey, Slater." Mr. Gilliard patted him on the back like a buddy, and Slater winced inwardly. "Having a good time?"

"Yeah. Everything's really nice." Slater answered politely.

"I'm Adam Laurence." Adam extended his hand to Mr. Gilliard. "Slater's brother."

Mr. Gilliard shook Adam's hand. "It's nice to meet you, Adam."

"Same here. Slater's told me a lot about you."

Slater looked mortified as Mr. Gilliard smiled.

"I can only hope that it wasn't all bad," Mr. Gilliard laughed.

"Not at all," Adam assured him, sounding very much like their father. "In fact, I think it's great that they're finally pumping some new blood into this place."

"Let's hope so." Mr. Gilliard appreciated the vote of confidence.

"I know this sounds crazy," Adam couldn't help staring at Mr. Gilliard as he poured a couple of glasses of wine. "But do we know each other? You look awfully familiar."

"Gee, I don't think so," Mr. Gilliard answered.

"By any chance, did you go to Brown?"

Mr. Gilliard shook his head. "No. I spent four glorious years trying to keep myself from getting thrown out of Princeton."

Adam laughed.

"Excuse me, please." Mr. Gilliard broke off the conversation. "I hate to rush off, but, unfortunately, I've got to get back over to Mrs. Kensington—the mother of one of my fifth-period freshmen—and assure her that I am qualified to be teaching her son. And that I am, in fact, older than Pookie."

Both Adam and Slater looked at him quizzically.

Mr. Gilliard gestured toward the little dog sitting

at Mrs. Kensington's feet. "Her cockapoo."

Even Slater had to laugh, in spite of himself.

"Anyway, it was really nice meeting you." Mr. Gilliard turned and headed off.

"How come you don't like the guy, Slater?" Adam asked. "He seems like an okay guy."

Slater shrugged uncomfortably. It was perfectly true that he didn't like Mr. Gilliard, but he would have had a hard time explaining to Adam why. Anyway, he didn't even feel like trying. He just hadn't realized his feellings were so obvious. He tried to get out of it.

"I never said I didn't like him," he said neutrally.

"You didn't have to. Slater, you never were very good at hiding your feelings, and you can't tell a good lie, either." This was all true, and who knew it better than Adam? "So how come? He's gotta be a big improvement over Spenguin."

"Yeah, maybe," Slater said offhandedly. "But things around here are never quite the way they seem."

CHAPTER · 16

When Trevor finally strolled out of Bowdin House, it was well past noon. He'd needed the sleep. The day before, he'd led his undefeated soccer team to one more victory. Later that night, he'd celebrated out on "Fantasy Island" with a little freshman girl whose name he couldn't remember. Trevor almost always celebrated with freshman girls. They were so easy to impress. They'd do almost anything just to wear his varsity jacket for awhile.

By the time he got up to Huntington Hall, the place was practically a mob scene. Trevor was always amazed at how many parents showed up for this extravaganza. He was sure his own parents were somewhere in the crowd, so busy socializing that they didn't notice his absence. He didn't bother looking for them but headed straight for the food. He wasn't about to face Trevor Senior and Cici on an empty stomach.

But Trevor barely had time to check out the food table when he saw the silver Mercedes station wagon turn onto the road. A Mercedes station wagon. Trevor just couldn't cope with the absurdity of that. It astounded to him that his old man could spend a small fortune on a car—and still end up looking like a geek.

His father's unexpected lateness distracted Trevor from his usual smug disdain of the man. He had never in his life known his father to be late for anything. It surprised Trevor. It surprised him to see that his mother was not in the car. And it surprised him to see his father pull into the circular driveway and double-park right in front of Huntington Hall.

If it had mattered at all to Trevor, he would have known immediately that something was wrong. But that didn't dawn on him until his father got out of the car, spotted Trevor across the lawn, and stalked toward him. Trevor recognized the look of disgust on his father's face. Still, he wasn't terribly concerned. He didn't even move to meet him. He stayed at the buffet table and continued eating as Trevor Senior approached.

"Trevor," his father said. It was a chilly greeting.

"Where's Mother?" Trevor ignored his father's mood.

"Your mother didn't come. And I won't be staying long, either."

Trevor was forced to acknowledge the situation. "Is something wrong?" He sounded more bored than concerned. Which he was.

His father just laughed a small and bitter laugh. "Oh, yes," he said finally. "Something is wrong. Something is *very* wrong."

Trevor just wanted to skip the boring buildup and cut to the chase. "What is it?"

"I've spoken to my friend who is on the admissions committee at Yale."

"And?" Trevor said with growing impatience.

"Congratulations," his father said with so much sarcasm that even Trevor couldn't mistake it for a compliment. "You have the dubious distinction of being the first Caldwell male ever rejected for admission to Yale."

"Oh, what a surprise," Trevor matched his father's sarcasm.

"Do you have any idea what this means to me?" This time there was real anguish in his father's voice.

"It means you're going to have to pull some strings. Just like you always do." Trevor buried his hands deep into his pockets and bowed his head a little, in an effort to look appropriately contrite. This was the point in the conversation where Trevor was supposed to show his father that he understood the error of his ways. They'd been through this drill so many times Trevor could do it in his sleep.

"Pull strings? At Yale? Surely you're joking. In order to be accepted to a school like that you have to demonstrate a capacity for excellence. At this point, it would be a great accomplishment for you to demonstrate a capacity for mediocrity."

That was a direct hit on Trevor's ego. "Good one," he said with a grimace. "You're way funny, Dad. A way funny guy."

"Yes. Thanks to you, Trevor, I have become quite a joke." His father wallowed in self-pity for a second. "You have thrown away generations of accomplishment, generations of tradition. You had no right to do this to me. No right and no reason."

"I didn't do anything to you. Why don't you try to remember: it's my life that we're talking about here. It's *my* life, Dad."

"Not until you start financing it," his father snapped, loud enough for a few heads to turn. Trevor Senior was oblivious to the people around them. His voice continued to rise. "And that may be sooner than you think. I've had it with you, Trevor. As of right now, I'm cutting you off."

"What's that supposed to mean?" It was a pointless question. Because Trevor knew very well what his father meant. His father was rolling out the big guns, and he was going to hurt Trevor real bad, in the only way that he could. He was going to cut his allowance—or maybe put a limit on his gold card.

Big deal. Trevor had a way around this, just like

he had a way around everything else. He'd just backdate an extra-big personal check and use that money to pad out the thin month. He'd wink at all the local merchants who were getting rich off his spending. And Trevor would be allowed to postdate charge receipts, too.

But what his father went on to say was like nothing Trevor had imagined. This time, he was well and truly being hung out to dry.

"I have cancelled all your credit cards. Should you try to use them, they will be confiscated and destroyed on the spot, on my specific orders. And I hope you have plenty of money left in your checking account, because I have no intention of adding to it. I will continue to pay for your education and your room and board. I still feel that is my responsibility. Unlike you, I live up to my responsibilities. But I will not put another penny in your pocket. I've made it too easy for you to be a party boy. As of right now, the party is over."

Trevor felt the bile rising in his throat. He thought for a moment he really might vomit from the force of the blow his father had just dealt him. He wanted more than anything to be able to strike back. He wished he had the nerve to actually hit the old man right in front of all the people who were watching them. And people were watching. It was part of what made this scene so humiliating for Trevor. But he was smart enough to control his anger, smart enough to know that hitting his father would serve no purpose, smart enough to know that his father had all the power. "I'm sorry, Dad." It was a desperate attempt to salvage his situation.

"No, my boy," Trevor Senior said coldly, his body ramrod straight and rigid. "I don't think you know what it is to be sorry." He turned his back on his son. "But you will." And he walked away, leaving his son standing alone in the crowd, too stricken to move.

♠ ♠ ♠

In the days that followed, this exchange between father and son would be misconstrued by all who witnessed it. All but one.

CHAPTER · 17

"No, my boy," Iggy Boy amused himself with the perfect imitation of Trevor's father. "I don't think you know what it is to be sorry." Iggy Boy laughed as he loaded the Nikon with a brand-new roll of film.

He'd been waiting for this, waiting to find just the right way to handle the situation. And now he had it. Now, thanks to Trevor Caldwell, Senior, getting rid of Junior was going to be a piece of cake.

Iggy Boy thought about sending the old man a thank-you note. In fact, he even wrote one. Iggy Boy got a real kick out of it. "Dear Sir, I'd like to extend my sincerest thanks to you for providing your son, Trevor, with the impetus to behave like a puerile little fool, thereby giving me the ability to 'cut him off' with even greater ease than you yourself have been able to achieve. Love and kisses to Cici. And all my best regards, Iggy Boy—the First and foremost."

Iggy Boy wasn't really going to send it. There was

no need to. In fact, Iggy Boy was quite sure that the note the Caldwells would receive—the note that Trevor would write himself—would be more than enough to provide the entire family with years of entertainment. But he *was* going to read it, just to Trevor, just for fun. Just so Trevor would know that he himself had provided Iggy Boy with the perfect solution for the perfect demise. And while he was sure he would have to explain the letter carefully, sure that Trevor couldn't possibly understand big words like *impetus* and *puerile*, Iggy Boy didn't mind. No. Trevor Caldwell would draw his last breath knowing that Iggy Boy was gonna walk away clean. Just like he always did.

It would all go down smoothly. As long as Iggy Boy didn't lose his temper . . . before the time was right . . . before he was sure that he and Trevor had total privacy. The walls in Bowdin House had ears . . . and Iggy Boy was not about to take any unnecessary chances. Nor was he about to ruin what was sure to be some of his best work.

He arranged the pictures he had taken of Trevor and Casey out on the island in chronological order so that he could show them to Trevor, one by one. One by one Iggy Boy would recapture the moments. Only this time, it would be Trevor—not Casey— who would look startled and uncomfortable and humiliated and bruised . . . in ways that Trevor

Caldwell didn't even know existed. And the only moment that wouldn't be recaptured was the moment Casey got to walk away. Because one thing was certain—Trevor Caldwell would definitely not walk away.

Iggy Boy put the pictures in his camera bag and checked the pockets to make sure there were at least a couple of extra rolls of film. Just in case. While thirty-six exposures generally supplied Iggy Boy with a good night's entertainment, he was counting on Trevor Caldwell to provide him with plenty of inspiration.

It wouldn't be long now. And Iggy Boy could already feel the surge of adrenaline that always accompanied the kind of photo shoot he had planned for Trevor. All he had to do was bide his time . . . and justice would finally be served.

"No, my boy," Iggy Boy said as he scanned all the pictures that covered the walls of his secret place. "You most definitely do not know what sorry is . . . but you will."

CHAPTER · 18

Chip held Trevor's head under the water as Trevor struggled in vain. Chip was by far the stronger of the two. Not only was he physically larger, he was also much more disciplined. On his best day Trevor couldn't have gotten away from Chip. But with what Chip figured was a half a bottle of vodka in him, Trevor put up a struggle that was nothing much more than a minor irritation.

Still, the risk of getting caught was high. And Chip couldn't allow that to happen. Trevor simply wasn't worth it. He pulled Trevor's head out of the water and got right up in his face. "Knock it off, will ya," he whispered through clenched teeth. "You're not making this any easier for either one of us." And as Trevor mumbled something incoherent, some plea for a quick and merciful death, Chip thrust his head back into the water. "Shut up," he said with contempt. Chip was tired and wet, and Trevor was working his very last nerve.

Oh, sure, it had been entertaining at first to watch Trevor beg and cry like a baby. It undeniably had been satisfying to see Trevor stripped of all his bravura. But it had worn thin too quickly. Trevor was all swagger and no substance, and even his pain seemed superficial..

Chip had had enough. He twisted the knob to turn off the shower and dragged Trevor—soaking wet—to the bathroom door. Chip checked to make sure the coast was clear. There would be hell to pay if Gilliard were to see Trevor in this condition.

Ever since the "Fantasy Island" incident, Chip had been longing to do something just like this to Trevor. But he wanted to do it to punish him—not to save his sorry butt from Mr. Gilliard. Still, it wouldn't be good for anyone if Trevor got caught so smashed. And Chip wanted to get his revenge when Trevor was sober—so he'd know exactly why he was getting what he had coming to him.

He managed to get Trevor to his room unseen, managed—with great difficulty—to get him into a pair of dry sweatpants and a T-shirt, and tried to make him lie down and sleep it off.

But Trevor didn't want to lie down and sleep it off. He wanted to feel sorry for himself, wanted to make Chip feel sorry for him. "Can you believe this," he moaned as he staggered back and forth across his room in a pathetic attempt at pacing. "I'm broke. Totally broke."

"Look, Trev, I'm tired. I've got to go to bed." Chip moved toward the door.

Trevor blocked him. "I don't think so, Chipster. I want some company."

"So what am I, your indentured servant?" Chip laughed at him.

"Pretty much," Trevor answered, a little belligerently.

"How do you figure?"

"Think about it, Chipster. In all the years I've been here, I haven't seen you pay for a single thing. I've paid for everything. I've financed you." Trevor was echoing his father, as if he could recover his pride by humiliating Chip the way his father had humiliated him. "The way I see it, you're bought and paid for. So the answer is, yeah, you pretty much *are* my indentured servant." Now it was Trevor who was laughing.

"Get out of my way." Chip tried to make it past him to the door, but Trevor planted himself in front of it.

"Walk out that door, and by tomorrow morning the whole school will know your pathetic little secret," Trevor threatened.

"What are you talking about?"

"That you're a total charity case." Trevor smiled maliciously when he saw the expression on Chip's face. "Did you honestly think I didn't know?

Chipster, let me tell you a little secret." He made like he was whispering, even though he could be heard all the way down the hall. "I can smell white trash a mile away. Yeah, I can just picture your old man, in a sleeveless t-shirt, polyester pants, a big gut, sitting in front of the TV, smashed out of his mind."

"Shut up," Chip growled.

"Let's be honest with one another, shall we, Chipster," Trevor slurred.

Chip hated it when drunks felt compelled to be "honest." That was usually just an invitation to fight.

"All this time you thought you were taking me to the cleaners," Trevor continued venomously. "But what was really happening was that I was buying you. You knew that was the deal as well as I did. Think about it, Chipster. You did what I wanted to do, went where I wanted to go. You even kept your mouth shut no matter what I did to your precious Casey. I'll bet if I'd wanted you to, you'd have even stood there and watched."

Chip couldn't even hear what Trevor was saying anymore. The blood rushed to his head like a hurricane. He had to get out of there before he did something stupid, something he would regret. In his need to escape, he pushed Trevor out of the way with such force that Trevor was lifted off the ground and flung across the room against the opposite wall. He hit hard and fell to the floor, unconscious.

Chip hoped he was dead. But he didn't bother to check because he knew it couldn't possibly be that easy. He just left to go back to his own room and compose himself enough to think it through and decide what he really was going to do about Trevor.

♠ ♣ ♠

When Trevor came to, he was momentarily startled by the sight of a figure sitting on his bed staring at him, until his eyes focused and he recognized who it was.

"What do you want now?" Trevor asked wearily, barely able to lift his head.

"Justice, you ignoble little worm."

Trevor laughed. It hurt his head. "At this hour?" He caught sight of his clock on the night table. It was nearly three in the morning. "You're out of your mind." He closed his eyes again, not realizing how true his statement was.

But that was because Trevor didn't know about Iggy Boy. Nobody did . . . until it was too late.

CHAPTER • 19

Trevor Caldwell hanging—dead—on "Fantasy Island," with the vacuum cord tied into a noose around his neck and wrapped around the thickest branch of the maple tree, was justice. Plain and simple. And Jake knew it.

But there was no way he was gonna share that information, no way at all. And so Jake just answered all the questions about Trevor Caldwell's death the same way he had about Cameron Wheeler's, like it was a tragedy—the way everyone else was saying it was, the way everyone else wanted to believe it was.

But that was a lie. And it wasn't the only one that Jake had to tell, because the vacuum cord that was found wrapped around Trevor's neck was the cord normally wrapped around the vacuum cleaner found in Jake's closet. The police asked Jake a couple of questions pertaining to the vacuum cleaner and its whereabouts. But those weren't the questions that bothered Jake. In fact, answering

questions about the vacuum cord and the whereabouts of the vacuum cleaner was real easy. After all,
Jake had already been through pretty much the
same line of questioning with Cameron Wheeler
and the garbage rope, so he knew just what to
expect. And the garbage rope questions had been a
whole lot trickier for Jake, being that Cameron
never left the maintenance closet. But the questions
about Jake's own whereabouts at the approximate
time that Trevor would have taken the vacuum
cord, and about whether or not Jake had seen him
do it, were a whole lot more bothersome.

Jake told the police that he hadn't seen a thing,
that he'd been in his own room, sound asleep. He
reminded the police of what they had pointed out to
him—that, after all it *was* three o'clock in the
morning they were talking about. At three o'clock in
the morning, where else was he gonna be? There
generally was no cleaning to be done at that hour.
And Jake assured the police that he always used that
time—that time of day that included three o'clock
in the morning—to get some sleep. He even
showed them where it was, his room, where he said
he had slept, the room behind the kitchen in the old
servant's quarters. And they believed him, believed
beyond a shadow of a doubt that Jake was telling
the truth—even though he wasn't.

Jake had never made it to his room—at least, not

the one behind the kitchen, and he'd never made it to sleep. At three o'clock in the morning in Bowdin House there was cleaning to be done, garbage to be put out. In the hours that followed Trevor's death, Jake hadn't been snoring up a storm, he'd been retching his guts up in the basement.

But the truth didn't matter, anyway. Because even before the police asked Jake any questions at all, they had already written off Trevor Caldwell's death the same way they had Cameron Wheeler's, as a suicide—just the way Jake knew they would.

Getting away with murder was the easiest thing in the world. Jake knew. Trevor Caldwell's death was an open-and-shut case. Just like they all were, all except Justin Taylor's. But Jake knew that case was closed, too. Only no one wanted to believe it. As far as they were concerned, Justin Taylor was a "runaway." It was what the police had said and what Justin's parents clung to—the idea that their little boy was just a runaway.

But Jake knew better. In fact, Jake felt pretty bad about the whole thing. Not about Justin—no, Jake didn't mind about not having to lay eyes on that boy ever again—but about his parents. After all this time, they were still looking for that boy, still believing that one day he'd be coming home.

Jake knew for a fact that when the school told his parents that Justin Taylor "checked out" before he disappeared, they weren't lying. Justin Taylor "checked out," all right. Only he was never coming back. Part of Jake wished he could tell Justin Taylor's parents that, just so they'd know. But he couldn't. No. Jake couldn't tell Justin Taylor's family the truth any more than he could tell Trevor Caldwell's or any of the others'. It would just stir up way too much trouble.

CHAPTER · 20

Mr. Gilliard had said they never had to talk about Trevor again. Unless Casey wanted to, unless she needed to talk to someone.

"I need to talk to someone," Casey said, standing in the doorway of Michael Gilliard's office on the first floor of Bowdin House.

"Of course, Casey," he said, looking up at her from behind his desk. "Come on in."

She did. And closed the door behind her.

"Sit down." He gestured to the chair across from him and she moved obediently to it. "Tell me what's bothering you."

"I don't even know where to begin," she said numbly. "This is just so terrible."

"This is about Trevor, isn't it?"

She nodded.

He nodded sympathetically. "It's a terrible thing when someone takes his own life, especially someone so young. And when it's someone you know, it brings out all kinds of confused feelings."

"Yes, it does, especially when your name is mentioned in the suicide note." It was the first time Casey had ever seen Mr. Gilliard look shocked.

"Casey, what are you talking about?"

"Trevor left a note. He talked about what happened out on the island. And about how sorry he was," her voice was cracking. "And how he'd never do anything like that again."

"Casey, how do you know this? I thought the contents of Trevor's note were to be kept private, just between the police and the family."

"I don't know what the rest of the note says, just the part about me. Trevor's parents sent a letter to the Headmaster and asked him to let me know how very sorry Trevor was for what he did, and how sorry they are, as well. Trevor's suicide was hard enough to deal with when I still hated him. But now— now, I guess *I'm* the one who's sorry."

Mr. Gilliard got up and came around the desk. He squatted down in front of her in order to make eye contact. Casey was reminded of her father, of the way he used to do the very same thing when she was little and had gotten hurt or was sad. She couldn't help feeling a little bit like a child again, small and helpless. But looking into Mr. Gilliard's eyes comforted her, made her feel as though there was someone there who was bigger, who would take care of everything.

"Casey, you can't blame yourself for what Trevor did. Apparently Trevor had just had a terrible fight with his father. But his father is no more to blame than you are. No matter what his father said to him, no matter how awful it was, it was no excuse for Trevor to kill himself. There is no excuse for that. Suicide is the ultimate act of selfishness and cowardice. And while it is a tragedy, a terrible tragedy, it's nobody's fault. Certainly not yours."

"It's just so awful to know that right before Trevor died, he was thinking about me." It was a terrible burden. She was angry with Trevor for leaving her with it, and angry with his parents, too. Then she felt guilty for being angry. Within seconds, her feelings were so confused that she didn't know *what* she felt anymore. But one thing was certain. She was about to burst into tears in front of Mr. Gilliard again.

And when she did, he put his arms around her and held her close. She rested her head against his chest and cried silently as he stroked her hair, consoling her. She listened to the strong and steady beating of his heart. It felt good. Too good. Without warning, comfort became pleasure. Casey was suddenly aware that Michael Gilliard felt exactly the way she'd wanted him to in her daydreams. And, even as she felt guilty about it, she wished this embrace would never end.

He moved his hand, put it under her chin and turned her face up so that she was looking into his eyes. Casey's breath caught. She was sure he was going to kiss her. And she wanted him to, so badly that she could feel it already. He moved closer— slowly, painfully slowly. It was as if he were fighting himself.

"Feeling a little better?" he asked in that even tone of voice.

Casey nodded, in a daze. She felt him let go of her, watched him stand up, and blushed at the wickedness of her own imagination.

"Do you mind if I open the door?" He waited for her to nod before he actually did. "We don't want anybody to misconstrue what's going on in here." He smiled as he went back to his own side of the desk.

Casey wondered what he meant by that. Did he think—know—that *she* had misconstrued it? Was he aware that she had a silly schoolgirl crush on him, delusions of romance? She was mortified by the thought and mortified by her behavior. "I'm so embarrassed," she apologized.

"You have no reason to be embarrassed," he said firmly and sincerely. "I'm flattered that you feel you can talk to me. I hope you'll continue to feel that way. We all need a shoulder to cry on now and then."

Casey managed a smile. But inside she was reeling in confusion. "I should go now." She stood up. "I have a class in a few minutes."

"Are you sure you're up to it? If not, I'll write you a note."

"No. I'd rather go. It'll give me something else to think about."

"All right, but if you need to talk some more, don't hesitate to come to me."

Never again, Casey thought. Her feelings for him were too strong. "Thank you," she managed to answer as she headed out the door, feeling foolish that she had imagined—even for a moment—that Mr. Gilliard's interest in her was any more than that of a good teacher for his student.

CHAPTER • 21

Iggy Boy watched Casey leave Mr. Gilliard's office. As he watched her make her way down the corridor, past the sitting room, through the front door, he had to fight the urge to grab her . . . to stop her . . . to keep her there . . . so that he could take her to his secret place . . . and really be alone with her . . . the way that Michael Gilliard had tried to be alone with her . . . and show her who it was that really cared . . . who it was that she could really count on . . . who it was that she could really trust.

Iggy Boy tried to fight the anger. He'd felt many things for Casey, but never anger. Never until now. He'd heard every word of what went on in Mr. Gilliard's office. And every word of it made him sick. He couldn't stand the fact that it was Mr. Gilliard that Casey ran to . . . Mr. Gilliard that Casey confided in . . . Mr. Gilliard that Casey cried to . . . and Mr. Gilliard that Casey wanted comfort from. Couldn't she see how totally incompetent he was? How totally useless?

Didn't she care that Mr. Gilliard had never even

bothered to question Trevor Caldwell . . . never even tried to confront him? Didn't she know what kind of man that made him? What kind of human waste he truly was? Didn't she find it insulting that, knowing full well the injustice that had been done, Michael Gilliard could sit there and call Trevor's death a "tragedy"? Didn't she know she deserved better than that?

Iggy Boy shook his head in disgust. Maybe he was wrong. Maybe Casey McCabe didn't deserve more than that. Maybe Iggy Boy was just wasting his time on her . . . just like he had wasted his time on the other one. Maybe Iggy Boy would end up giving . . . and giving . . . and giving . . . and getting nothing in return . . . just like he had before. Maybe Casey McCabe was no different. Maybe Casey McCabe would try to humiliate him the same way the other one had tried to humiliate him. Maybe Casey McCabe wanted to be treated like dirt . . . maybe she really wanted someone like Mr. Gilliard . . . maybe she really wanted an ignominious piece of scum . . .

And maybe Iggy Boy would see to it that Casey never had the chance to prove him wrong . . . never had the chance to break his heart. Once had been enough . . . and it was only once. And Iggy Boy had sworn that no one would ever do that to him again . . . no one would ever hurt him like that . . . betray him like that again . . . humiliate him like that again.

Iggy Boy had to calm down . . . his emotions were taking control, and he knew it. There was nothing logical about the way he was feeling, nothing rational. He had to put things in perspective. He had no right to be angry with Casey . . . no right at all. She had done nothing to hurt him—at least not directly . . . and she'd done nothing to betray him, nothing to humiliate him. The fact was that she didn't know about Iggy Boy . . . didn't know that he was the one that she should run to and confide in . . . and cry to . . . and be comforted by, didn't know that Iggy Boy was the one that would be there for her . . . always. She had no one else to turn to, no where else to go.

Iggy Boy quickly turned the anger he was feeling in the direction it belonged . . . toward Mr. Gilliard. After all, it was Mr. Gilliard who had taken advantage of the situation, Mr. Gilliard who used Trevor Caldwell's "suicide"—which Iggy Boy had orchestrated so beautifully and so thoughtfully—as a way to ingratiate himself. How dare he sit there pretending to be so full of concern, so full of compassion? What a farce. If he were so concerned and so compassionate . . . it would have been him, not Iggy Boy, who assisted in Trevor Caldwell's "tragic suicide."

Enough was enough. Iggy Boy had to make a move. He had to find a way to get close to Casey . . . and he had to find a way to get rid of Mr. Gilliard.

CHAPTER · 22

It was a beautiful day—late spring—and everything was in full bloom—like it was summer—and Jake was at the lake, the one his granddaddy used to take him to—and he was just a boy, just eight years old—and he was sitting in his favorite spot, under the big old maple tree, the one he carved his name into—and he was fishing with the pole his granddaddy made for him, and he was so happy—the way he always was when he was fishing with his granddaddy.

Jake loved his granddaddy more than anyone or anything in the whole world. He was the only family Jake had ever had. His mama had died when he was just a baby. Jake had never had a father, not one that he knew of, anyway. And "Moms"—that's what Jake's granddaddy called his grandmother—had died long before Jake was ever born. Granddaddy never took another wife, always said that he was too old for that and, anyway, he loved "Moms" way too much for that. He loved Jake way too much for that.

Jake walked to the bank of the lake and cast out his line just the way his granddaddy had taught him to. It went out real far, just the way it was supposed to. And his granddaddy patted him on the back, just the way he always did, and he said, "You're a good boy, Jake—a real good boy." Jake smiled a real, big smile, just the way he always did when he knew his granddaddy was proud of him. Before he knew it Jake felt something tugging on the line and he was real excited.

But when he turned around to get his granddaddy's attention—there were men. A lot of men, bad men, like ghosts. They grabbed Jake's granddaddy and held him down so they could beat on him. And they were calling his granddaddy all kinds of terrible names—saying that he was a liar and a thief. Only none of it was true. And Jake's granddaddy was screaming. Screaming for Jake to run, screaming for Jake to get away. Pleading with the men to leave Jake out of it. But Jake couldn't run: Jake couldn't do anything at all to help his granddaddy. And the men were laughing. Laughing at Jake. Laughing at the way he looked. Laughing at how scared he was. Laughing the entire time they were wrapping the rope around his granddaddy's throat, talking about how justice was being served . . .

All of a sudden Jake wasn't at the lake anymore. He was on "Fantasy Island." But he was still fishing—which didn't make any sense at all, 'cause there were no good eatin' fish in the lake surrounding the island. And Jake was still a little boy. Only somehow he knew that he wasn't really. Somehow he knew that he was at Huntington Prep—that he worked at Huntington Prep—that he was a man now. But Jake was still seeing himself as a child . . .

There was a tug on line, just like before. Only this time Jake wasn't excited. This time, Jake was scared. And this time, Jake was all alone. He called for his granddaddy, but his granddaddy wasn't there. No one was there. But the voices were there. Screaming at Jake. Laughing at Jake. Calling Jake "ignorant."

Jake wanted to let go of the fishing pole and run, but he couldn't. It was like the pole was glued to his hands. The line was reeling itself in, and Jake couldn't stop it. Whatever it was on the other end of the line was big—bigger than any fish in any lake could possibly be . . .

Suddenly the line caught, and for a split second Jake felt relieved. Until the body started to surface.

The body of that pretty little girl, the one that Jake liked so much. Only now she was all blue and swollen. Jake couldn't bear the sight of her, not again. He should have know better. He should have known how much trouble she was gonna cause.

Jake woke up in a sweat. It took him a minute to realize where he was, to realize that it all was just a dream, that it wasn't happening, not for real. It couldn't have been, because this time he was in his room, the one behind the kitchen, the one he had told the police he'd been sleeping in the night Trevor died.

Jake reached under the mattress for the bottle of Jack Daniels he kept there. As he took a healthy swig, he thought about Casey being in Bowdin House, being with Mr. Gilliard. A chill ran up his spine—the kind of chill that his granddaddy swore meant something bad was gonna happen.

CHAPTER · 23

Trevor's death provided Chip with more comfort than he'd ever known at Huntington. As Trevor's best friend Chip was the recipient of a great outpouring of condolences on his loss. He found himself treated—by students and teachers alike—with understanding and deference. All he had to do was act bereaved and any behavior became excusable. Trevor turned out to be almost as useful dead as he'd been alive.

Chip took full advantage of the situation. The only thing that made him feel guilty was Casey. She believed he was hurting just as sincerely as everybody else believed it. During the memorial service at the school chapel, Casey had sat beside him and held his hand the whole time. He'd loved the feel of her so close to him, the warmth of her hand in his. But it was also painfully unsatisfying because it was happening under false pretenses.

He wished he could touch her for real. He wished he could tell her how he felt about her, how he'd always felt about her. Someday he would. Someday, when he'd made everything just right. Until then, he would just stay close to her, and watch over her, and imagine.

"Earth to Chip." Casey's voice brought him out of his fantasy.

She'd come in and taken her seat beside him without his having noticed. He wondered how long she'd been trying to get his attention.

"Where were you?" she asked when his eyes met hers.

He couldn't tell her the truth. "Nowhere. Just zoned out, I guess."

"Did you finish your paper?"

"Yeah," he nodded, still trying to compose himself.

"So who'd you do?"

For a minute he didn't understand the question.

"Which character did you write about?" She clarified it, patiently.

"Right." He hesitated. He had to look down at his paper to find the answer. "Ishmael. How about you?"

"Queequeg."

"Who?"

"The Indian," she reminded him.

"Oh, yeah. Right."

"Chip, did you read this book?"

"Some of it," he confessed conspiratorially as Mr. Gilliard entered the room.

"Good morning," Mr. Gilliard said brightly, the way teachers always do when there's a test or a paper due. "I've got some good news and some bad news."

Chip noted with envy the way Casey looked at Mr. Gilliard. No question about it; she had a thing for him. And if Chip had to lay money on it, he'd bet that Gilliard had a thing for her, too. It was just another reason to hate the guy.

"First, the bad news," Mr. Gilliard continued. "Your papers are due today."

After the class made it clear that that was a lame joke, Eddie Brewster asked, "So what's the good news?"

"The good news is that after I collect them, you are free to leave. A free period as a reward for a job well done."

That brought murmurings of approval. Papers were produced in a hurry as Mr. Gilliard moved among the rows collecting them. He continued talking as he went.

"I am counting on the fact that they are well done. Because, as I explained before, most of your grade for this semester depends on the quality of this paper."

Mr. Gilliard took Casey's paper, then Chip's.

"If you didn't understand that, I'm still willing to cut you some slack. I'll be reading these papers this weekend. If you have second thoughts about the work you've done, you have until Sunday night to come and talk to me or even give me a rewrite. I want to see you all do well in this class. Of course, the one unforgivable sin is plagiarism—passing off someone else's work as your own. I know you probably think I'm old and out of touch, but I am well aware of the black-market term-paper trade. And I'm pretty familiar with what's available on *Moby Dick*."

Chip was sure he was bluffing.

"In fact," Mr. Gilliard wanted to prove that he was not bluffing, "there's an excellent paper—A+ guaranteed, if the teacher's never seen it before— that starts 'My name is Ishmael. But you don't have to call me that.'"

Chip didn't hear another word that Mr. Gilliard said. He sat there stunned by the recitation of the first two lines of his paper. And he continued sitting there even after the other students and Mr. Gilliard had filed out of the room.

Casey didn't leave with the rest of them but waited until everyone was gone. She asked, "What's wrong?"

"I'm screwed," was all he could manage.

"What do you mean?"

"I paid fifty bucks for that paper," he said in disbelief, talking more to himself than to her.

"Oh Chip, you *didn't*."

Her disappointment in him was almost as hard to take as the reality of his situation. "I'm screwed," he repeated. "Totally screwed."

"You've got to do something. There's got to be some way to fix it," Casey tried to encourage him.

Chip couldn't believe Casey's ability to forgive him almost anything. "There's no way to fix it. You heard him. They can throw you out of school for plagiarism if you get caught. And he'll do it to me. He'll get me thrown out of here, and he'll probably enjoy doing it. I won't get into college. And then . . ." he trailed off, thinking of what his life would be without college, without football. What would he do? Go back to where he came from? Stay there the rest of his life, with no chance of escape? "Totally screwed," he said hopelessly.

"Mr. Gilliard's not like that."

She was trying to make Chip feel better, but it made him sick to hear her glorifying Gilliard. He wished that Casey could feel for him what he knew she felt for Mr. Gilliard. Chip knew that Casey loved him like a brother, loved him in spite of all his shortcomings, but it wasn't enough anymore. Chip wanted more.

"You should go and talk to him," Casey persisted.

Chip didn't say anything.

"I'll talk to him if you want," she offered.

"No." Chip couldn't stand the thought of that, even though he knew it would probably work. If Casey asked, Gilliard would probably let Chip off the hook, just to impress Casey with what a wonderful guy he was. But Chip couldn't allow that. He wouldn't provide the reason for Casey to be alone—behind closed doors—with Gilliard.

There were other ways to handle this. Chip knew exactly what he had to do, and he knew he had to move fast.

"What are you going to do?"

"I don't know," Chip lied. "But promise me you won't say anything to Mr. Gilliard. And promise me you won't say anything to anybody else, either."

She was hesitant in her agreement. But Chip never doubted for one second that Casey, having made the promise, would keep one more of his secrets.

CHAPTER · 24

Slater waited just around the corner from the American Lit classroom. He wanted to catch Casey on her way out. Everyone else had gone, everyone but Chip. Slater wondered what the two of them were doing alone in that room. He'd always known that there was something going on between Chip and Casey, some special relationship, but he could never figure out exactly what it was. He was almost positive that it wasn't romantic, but, still, he couldn't help feeling jealous.

Finally they emerged, Chip heading off in one direction, Casey in another. Slater stayed right where he was, out of sight, until Chip was well on his way. Only then did he pursue Casey, hurrying up beside her. She was lost in her own thoughts—clearly not pleasant ones—and she was startled by Slater's sudden appearance.

"You scared me half to death," she gasped.

"I'm sorry." He meant it. "I didn't mean to. I just wanted to give you something." He held out a manila envelope to her.

"What's this?" She smiled as she took the envelope.

"Pictures. The ones I took on Parents' Day."

That certainly excited her. She couldn't open the envelope fast enough.

"The one you took of my father and me?"

Slater nodded, pleased with himself. Whatever was troubling her before was gone now.

"How did it turn out?" She finished the question just as she saw the picture.

"You tell me," he answered. But her face said it all.

"Oh Slater, this is wonderful! It's the nicest picture anyone's ever taken of the two of us. You are so talented!"

He smiled at the compliment. "I had a perfect subject."

"My father is going to love this."

"I made two prints." He'd really made three. "One for your father and one for you." And one for himself.

"Thank you so much," she said, finding the second print sandwiched between two pieces of cardboard underneath the first. There was also a third picture.

"That's for your father," he said as she looked at the picture of herself alone. "Tell him he was right, it *will* be the prettiest picture in the yearbook. Tell him I've seen them all, and I can guarantee it."

"I can't believe my father said that to you. It's so embarrassing."

"It's true, Casey." Slater didn't know where he'd found the courage to say out loud what he'd been feeling for so long.

Casey fumbled self-consciously for something to say. "Thank you," she said simply, graciously.

They stood there for an awkward moment as Casey slid the pictures back into the envelope. Then Slater decided that as long as he had gone this far out on a limb with her, he might as well take his brother's advice and finish it. "Next Saturday night is the Mischief Night dance at Bowdin House. Would you like to go with me?"

She looked surprised. For a moment, Slater felt as though he'd made a terrible error in judgment. He was furious with himself for having blurted it out just like that, for being so clumsy about it. He should have eased into it more gracefully, should have tested the waters before jumping in with both feet. But now it was too late. Now he'd put Casey on the spot. She was probably struggling to find a way to let him down easy, because she was too nice a person to just blow him off. But no matter how gracefully she turned him down, it was going to be humiliating. And it was going to hurt.

"Sure," she answered, her face lighting up with a radiant smile, "that would be nice."

Slater had been so ready for rejection that it took a moment for him to realize that she'd actually said yes. "Great!" He reacted finally, but he couldn't think of anything else to say, and again there was an awkward silence.

It was Casey who broke it this time. "I think I should probably head over to the library and do some studying."

"Well, then, I guess I'll see you later."

"Right," she said. "See you later."

Slater watched her walk away, wondering what it would be like—an evening with Casey McCabe, in the flesh instead of in a photograph. It would either be the best night of his life . . . or the worst.

CHAPTER · 25

"Didn't I tell you?" Margo gloated. As usual she was just a little too loud, and the librarian shot her yet another warning look and a sharp "shh." "This is going to be the beginning of a beautiful relationship," she lowered her tone, but not her enthusiasm.

"It's a party, Margo," Casey tried to sound casual about it. "Not a lifetime commitment."

"I can't believe Slater finally, finally asked you to go out with him."

"Tell me about it—I was there, and I can hardly believe it myself. It was so out of the blue." Casey really was still surprised that Slater had asked her out and still didn't know what to make of it. But she wouldn't allow herself to buy into Margo's romantic notions.

"What *exactly* did he say to you?" Margo wanted to hear every single detail—ten times.

"I told you, he said, 'Next Saturday night is the Mischief Night dance at Bowdin House. Would you like to go with me?'"

"And you said yes!" Margo could barely contain her excitement.

"What else could I say?"

"You could have said no." Margo could not be shaken in her ideas about where this one, simple date would lead.

"How could I have said no? It's not like I had something else to do. There was no reason to say no to him. *And* he had just given me these pictures— for my father."

"And?" Margo wanted to hear another reason.

"And what?"

"*And* you like him. Admit it, you like him, too."

There was no way to disagree with Margo. "Of course I like him. He's a very nice guy," Casey said matter-of-factly, unromantically.

"And good-looking," Margo goaded.

"Yes, he is good-looking," Casey admitted.

"And smart."

"And smart," Casey agreed.

"And totally perfect for you!"

Casey gave up. It was no use trying to protest. Margo was going to believe just what she wanted to believe—that Slater and Casey were destined to be together, that they were a perfect match. But Casey wasn't at all convinced that they were a perfect match. She wasn't even convinced that they could make it through one date together. "He's so quiet," she voiced her main concern about spending an entire evening with Slater.

"He's shy," Margo explained.

"Especially with girls."

"That's because he had that girlfriend who did a real number on him."

"He did?" Casey didn't remember any girlfriend.

"It was right after our sophomore year. I told you about it." Margo's family and Slater's family had summer homes not far from one another. "She was a little witch."

"So what happened?" Casey was curious.

"I don't know exactly, except that she dumped him—real hard. And it really messed him up. But that's ancient history. All that matters now is that you're going to the Mischief Night dance with Slater, and now I have to make sure I get an invitation so that I'll be there to see just what kind of mischief the two of you get into," Margo teased.

"Oh, please." Casey rolled her eyes.

"The problem is," Margo went on, thinking out loud, "I never go to parties at Bowdin House because of all the animals that live there. So I've already blown off the guys who've asked me. But the party's invitation-only, so who am I going to get to invite me? Life is *so* complex!"

"I'll bet Eddie Brewster and David Cross don't have dates yet," Casey laughed. The idea of Margo accepting a date with either one of them was unthinkable.

"I'll bet they don't," Margo said with certainty. "So which one should I go with, Tweedledum or Tweedledumber?"

"You can't be serious," Casey gasped. The last time Eddie Brewster asked Margo for a date, she'd told him that she'd rather jump into the lion cage at the zoo wearing a pork-chop bikini.

"It's a party, not a lifetime commitment," Margo parroted Casey's own words. "Besides, I wouldn't miss this for the world."

CHAPTER · 26

At twelve-thirty in the afternoon, nearly the entire population of Huntington Prep was to be found in the main dining room in Huntington Hall. From twelve-thirty until one-thirty each day, everything and everybody stopped for lunch. The school's population was small enough, and the dining room large enough, that everyone could be accommodated at one time. The administration felt that it was a good opportunity for students and faculty to mix and mingle.

Chip took the opportunity to do something else.

At twelve-thirty in the afternoon, Bowdin House was deserted. Even Jake was usually up at Huntington Hall, having his lunch in the kitchen with the rest of the help. There wasn't a soul to be found in Bowdin House. And that was exactly the way Chip wanted it.

He wouldn't need the full hour to accomplish his task. In fact, he was hoping that ten or fifteen minutes would be enough time. Then he would be in the dining room with everyone else, enjoying his lunch, a huge load off his mind.

It was a simple solution to a stupid problem. Chip was surprised that he hadn't thought of it immediately. But he chalked that up to his preoccupation with Gilliard and Casey.

The door to Mr. Gilliard's office was closed. Chip tried the knob, but it was locked. He'd assumed it would be. Normally he would have knocked before trying the knob. But this time, there was no reason. There was no chance that Gilliard was inside. Chip had watched him leave Bowdin House ten minutes earlier.

The locks on all the doors in Bowdin House were practically useless, the kind that could be popped with just a file—or a credit card. And it just so happened that Chip had a credit card. Trevor Caldwell's. Yeah, Chip was certainly going to miss old Trev—he'd definitely had his uses.

Chip slipped the card between the door and the jamb, and the lock popped easily. Then he stepped inside and closed the door behind him. Once inside, he proceeded to ransack the office as deftly as a professional burglar.

He found Mr. Gilliard's briefcase containing the term papers on the floor of the closet. Perfect. All he had to do was steal his paper and play dumb when Gilliard realized that he didn't have it. Chip would remind him that he'd handed it in. Surely Gilliard would remember that. That would buy Chip a few days before Gilliard asked him for a replacement paper, enough time to actually write one, or pay someone else to do it for him.

As he knelt down on the floor to open the briefcase, something caught his attention—something odd. But he ignored it, intent on the task at hand. It was only when he'd found his paper, when he was confident that he'd saved himself from expulsion—and done it with forty-five minutes to spare—that he allowed himself to be distracted by what had caught his eye.

At the back of the closet there was another door. Chip pushed aside the briefcase containing the papers, including his own, and stood up to try the door. The knob turned, but the door was stuck, almost as though it had been painted shut. Using his on-the-job football training, Chip expertly rammed it with his shoulder. It gave.

The door opened to a narrow staircase. There was not enough light to see very far up. Chip reached into his pocket and pulled out a silver lighter, another posthumous gift from Trevor.

In the light of the flame Chip could see that the staircase was ancient. It was probably the service staircase from the days when Bowdin House was a private residence. From the looks of it, the stairs hadn't been used since then, either. The steps were thickly furred with dust, and the walls were criss-crossed with cobwebs.

Wanting to know where the stairs went, Chip decided he had plenty of time to find out. Brushing the sticky webs aside, he followed them all the way up to the second floor, where there was a small landing and a door frame. But there was no door, no access to the floor. He could picture the panelled wall from the other side. It was the end of the second-floor hallway. He'd never imagined that there was a staircase or anything else behind that wall. He knew without continuing that the third and fourth floors would be the same, that for some reason the staircase had been closed off. But he kept climbing anyway, curious to see where it ended. He followed it all the way up and was surprised to find a doorway still intact—and light coming into the stairwell from under the door.

Chip hadn't ever given it much thought, but he realized now that he'd never known Bowdin House had an attic. Of course, he should have known it was there: as he thought about it, he could picture the dormer windows above the fourth floor. But he couldn't remember ever having seen any other access to an attic, or ever hearing about an attic. And he would have—if there'd been one. He imagined that, like the stairs that led to it, the attic hadn't been used in many, many years.

But Chip was mistaken, because when he forced this door, he found himself standing in a dorm room. It took his eyes a minute to adjust to the bright sunlight pouring through the window. But it took his brain even longer to adjust to what he was seeing. A dorm room. Not a real one, but an almost perfect facsimile. The walls were makeshift. And the furniture was old and and beat-up, like the furniture Chip had seen Jake cart out for garbage, furniture that definitely came from Bowdin House. Despite its shabbiness, the room was meticulously neat. The bed was made so tightly that Chip was sure he could bounce a quarter on it—if only he weren't way too scared to even try. The desk was in perfect order; a blotter in the middle, a fancy pen and pencil set above it, a dictionary and a thesaurus to the right, and a neat stack of school papers to the left. Despite the oppressive neatness, the room appeared cluttered—because of the photographs that covered every wall.

Very clearly, someone lived in this room. But if that was true, how did that person gain access? Certainly not the way Chip had entered. There were no other doors, only the window, which was large enough for someone to fit through comfortably. But it was also fifty feet from the ground. Chip moved to the window, curious to see if entry were at all possible. When he looked out, he discovered that it was not only possible but very likely that someone had been coming and going in exactly that way. There were footprints on the ledge leading to the fire escape that ran down the side of the building. Someone had been using this room. Regularly. But who?

From the window Chip had a wonderful view of the east side of the campus. He could even see "Fantasy Island." More importantly, he could see that no one was approaching Bowdin House. He was free to snoop around a little longer.

His attention was drawn to the pictures on the walls. At first glance, they told little. Except for their fanatical orderliness—names and dates carefully recorded beneath each shot—like yearbook pictures.

The first name he saw was Justin Taylor's. The first picture in the row showed Justin Taylor sitting at his desk in his dorm room. It was a yearbook-type picture, as was the one next to it, and the one next to that. Chip's eyes scanned the row of pictures of Justin Taylor all the way to the end, to the very last picture. The picture of Justin Taylor in a shallow grave.

Chip couldn't believe what he was seeing. It had to be some kind of horrible joke. His eyes began darting back and forth over the rows and rows of other people, people who at first were smiling, living—then not smiling—on their knees, pleading into the camera . . . then . . . unbelievable, macabre.

He saw Cameron Wheeler—hanging in the closet, his eyes bulging, his tongue hanging out of his mouth, grotesquely long. And Spenguin, dead in the stairwell. And Trevor, hanging from the tree on the island. And all the others. There were car accidents and skiing accidents and boating accidents and subway accidents and suicides . . . and things Chip couldn't—and didn't care to—identify.

But it was the pictures of the girl that very nearly made him lose control. When Chip saw Casey's face among the others, he felt as though his chest had caved in. He found himself struggling for breath and not able to get any. It felt as though an elephant were standing on his chest. The lack of oxygen made him light-headed. For a moment he thought he might black out. And he half-wished he *would* black out, because the reality was too horrible, too incomprehensible.

Only fear snapped him out of it, that primal fear that triggers the instinct for survival. If he blacked out here, his picture was sure to end up on the wall with all the others.

He forced himself to look at the girl again. And he realized that it was not Casey, just someone who looked a whole lot like her. And someone who, in the very last picture at the end of the row, was most certainly dead—just like all the others. He felt sorry for her, even though he didn't know her. He was just grateful that it wasn't Casey.

But there *were* pictures of Casey, more pictures of Casey than of all the others combined. They were on the wall behind Chip, the wall directly over the bed. He found those when he turned away from the other girl, the girl who looked so much like Casey. This time, Chip knew that there was no mistake, as he looked with a terrible sense of dread. They were not pictures for which Casey posed. They were too candid for Casey to have been aware that she was being photographed, except for one shot—a picture of Casey and her father.

Chip was suddenly more afraid for Casey than he was for himself. She was being stalked by a maniac. And Chip had to find out who it was. He looked out the window again to make sure that no one was coming, and checked his watch to make sure he still had time. Then he continued his search of the room.

He found nothing of a personal nature, nothing to identify the inhabitant. The room itself was not really lived-in, simply kept by someone who was living a life apart from this. Even the papers on the desk offered no clue. Suicide notes, newspaper clippings, and the letter to Trevor's father—the letter signed "Iggy Boy." But that name meant nothing to Chip, except that it sounded ridiculous, laughable. But Chip didn't laugh. There was nothing funny about someone capable of doing what Iggy Boy was capable of doing.

He wondered what he was going to do. He certainly couldn't tell anybody. What would he say, that he'd broken into Gilliard's office and found this place while he was snooping around? And even if he could think of a better story, who would he tell? "Iggy Boy" could be anybody.

Chip was looking out the window again, checking to be sure that no one was coming. Then he realized how to find out who was using this room. He would have to find a place where he could keep an eye on the window, because he was sure that that was how Iggy Boy came and went.

But Chip was wrong. Behind him a floor panel slid open, and Iggy Boy entered his secret place.

CHAPTER · 27

Chip Cimino was in big, big trouble. And Michael Gilliard had no idea what he was going to do about it. He tossed Chip's paper onto the coffee table, got up from the couch and went into the kitchen to get himself some aspirin.

He'd had a blinding migraine since lunchtime, and he couldn't seem to shake it. Even the unplanned nap at his desk in his English Department office hadn't helped. And the aspirin wouldn't, either. But he popped a few anyway and went back to the couch to lie down. He was just going to have to ride it out, like he always did.

The doctor said it was stress—nothing serious, not a brain tumor or an aneurysm. Michael Gilliard *was* stressed. He wanted very much to prove his worth at Huntington, both as a teacher and as a House Master. Neither job was particularly easy. And Chip Cimino wasn't helping one bit. Chip Cimino had committed the one unforgivable sin.

He picked up Chip's paper again, hoping that

when he looked at it this time, it would read differently. But the miracle didn't happen. The paper still began, "My name is Ishmael. But you don't have to call me that." He didn't have to read any more. He could practically recite this paper by heart. That was because Michael Gilliard had written it—almost ten years before. And he'd gotten an A on it. Over the years, so had a lot of other students.

Michael Gilliard didn't know when or how the paper had made it onto the black market. He had to admit that when he'd first found out about it, he'd been pretty impressed with himself. He'd been even more impressed when a colleague told him that his paper had turned up as far away as California. It had seemed flattering and amusing—until one of his own students handed that paper in to him. Now, it was only cheating.

When he heard the knock on his door, he hoped it was Chip. And he knew that if it was, and if Chip was duly sorry, he would find a way to handle the situation that didn't include the Honor Council or Chip's expulsion.

But it wasn't Chip. It was Jake to whom he opened the door.

"Evenin', Mr. Gilliard, sir."

"Jake, I would really appreciate it if you would just call me 'Michael.'"

"Sorry, sir, I can't do that. It just wouldn't be appropriate."

What didn't seem appropriate to Michael Gilliard was the idea of a man more than twice his age addressing him as "sir." "Even when it's just the two of us?"

"Even then, Mr. Gilliard."

Michael Gilliard wondered whether Jake insisted on formality as a way of keeping his distance, or if it was just an unbreakable habit cultivated by years of oppression under Mr. Spegman. Either way, it was obviously hopeless to try to change it.

"What can I do for you, Jake?"

"I was up here cleaning your room for you earlier this afternoon."

Jake had the master key that let him into all the rooms so that he could clean them.

"Dustin' and what-not," he rambled on. "But I didn't get a chance to vacuum. Not because I was bein' lazy or nothin'. Just didn't have the new vacuum cleaner yet. Can't imagine how it took better than a week for me to get a new vacuum cleaner, but it did. I'm not bein' ungrateful, mind you, 'cause this new vacuum cleaner is a real fine machine. Lots of power, much better than the other one. But I'm ashamed to say that these carpets are filthier than they've ever been. And I want to take care of that as quick as I can. No use puttin' off 'til tomorrow what you can do today. I hope you don't mind. It'll just take me a couple of minutes, and I'll have these rugs cleaned up the way they ought to be."

Michael Gilliard's head was killing him. The last thing he wanted to do was put up with the noise of a vacuum cleaner. But he smiled and nodded, and let Jake in, because he couldn't bear to stand in the way of Jake's performance of the duties he took so seriously. "Sure, Jake. I don't mind at all."

"I really appreciate that, Mr. Gilliard, sir."

The minute Jake turned the vacuum on, Michael realized that there was no way his head could take the noise—not even for a couple of minutes. "Jake!" He waved his hand to get Jake's attention. Jake shut off the vacuum. "Listen, I think I'm gonna go downstairs for awhile."

"You don't have to do that, sir, I can work around you."

Michael Gilliard smiled. "I know you can, Jake. But I think I'm gonna go down to my office. I've got a lot of papers to read anyway."

"I can sure see that." Jake nodded toward the pile of term papers lying on the table in front of the sofa.

"That way you can take your time, and I can get some work done." Michael Gilliard picked up the papers on the table and put them into his briefcase. "Just lock up when you're finished." He headed for the door.

"You know I will, Mr. Gilliard, sir." Jake noticed a paper on the sofa. He picked it up. "Mr. Gilliard," Jake got his attention. "You forgot this one." Jake held the paper out.

Michael Gilliard walked back to Jake, and took the paper. "Thanks, Jake," he said as he looked at the title page. "Casey's." He said out loud, not really to Jake.

"'Scuse me?"

"The paper. It belongs to a student of mine named Casey." Despite the pain of the headache, his face lit up. "I've actually read this one," he said as he put it into his briefcase with the others. "Twice. It's the best work I've seen in a long time. I only wish I had more students like her." He couldn't help but notice the way Jake was suddenly staring at him . . . almost through him . . . and looking a bit shaken up. "Is something wrong, Jake?"

Jake shook his head.

"You sure?"

Jake pulled his eyes away. "No, sir, nothing's wrong. I just want to get to my vacuuming, that's all."

Michael Gilliard knew Jake was lying. He could see clearly that Jake wasn't feeling right, but he didn't want to push it. He knew Jake drank now and again, and he figured that maybe Jake was just feeling the effects of another binge. He had no intention of making an issue of it—no intention of humiliating him. "Sure thing, Jake." Michael Gilliard headed for the door. "I'll be in my office if anybody needs me."

And with that, he headed out, leaving Jake alone to do his cleaning up.

CHAPTER · 28

"Evenin', Mr. Gilliard, sir." Jake greeted Mr. Gilliard as he opened the door to his quarters.

"Jake, I would really appreciate it if you would call me 'Michael.'"

"Sorry, sir, I can't do that. It just wouldn't be appropriate."

"What kind of ignorance has taken hold of you now, Michael?" Mr. Spegman brayed. He was standing behind Mr. Gilliard at the doorway. "Informality is totally inappropriate and will not be tolerated. Isn't that right, Jake?"

Jake could barely answer. He was totally unnerved by the sight of Mr. Spegman . . . looking very dead . . . and all broken up, just like he looked after the fall. And Jake was sure he was dead, only he was still afraid of him . . . still afraid of the consequences of not answering the man. "Yes, sir, Mr. Spegman, sir. Sure is."

"What can I do for you, Jake?" Mr. Gilliard asked casually . . . like he didn't even see Mr. Spegman . . .

didn't hear Jake talkin' to Mr. Spegman. Didn't see him standing there, dead.

"I just want to vacuum up, sir. Didn't have a chance to get to it before."

"Indolence is unforgivable, Jake." Mr. Spegman admonished him.

"No, sir, Mr. Spegman, sir," Jake was starting to feel nervous. "I wasn't bein' lazy . . . I just didn't have my new vacuum yet."

"Come on in, Jake." Mr. Gilliard opened the door to him.

"Yes, Jake," Mr. Spegman pulled Jake by the arm right past Mr. Gilliard, who didn't seem to notice. "Do come in. There are some people here I'm sure you would enjoy seeing—again."

Mr. Spegman pushed Jake into Mr. Gilliard's quarters with the same kind of force that had pushed Mr. Spegman himself down the stairs of the field house. "Don't be ignorant, Jake," Mr. Spegman said pompously. "Say hello."

"Hey, Jake." Cameron Wheeler was sitting on the sofa—with the garbage rope still tied around his neck, looking just as dead as he had hanging in the maintenance closet. "How's it hanging?"

"Yeah, Jake," Trevor Caldwell laughed. "How is it hanging?" He was standing right behind Jake, pulling on the vacuum cord that was still wrapped around his throat. "Chipster sends his regards. He's a little late. That happens sometimes with the new arrivals."

Jake looked around the room. Justin Taylor was there, all covered with mud . . . and Matthew Ewing . . . and Jonathan Parker . . . and all the others. Faces that Jake wanted to forget about—faces that Jake had never wanted to have to look at again.

"Hey, Jake, your little girlfriend is here." Cameron Wheeler taunted. "Only she's in the tub—floating."

Everyone in the room laughed. Everyone but Mr. Gilliard, who seemed to be going about his business like there was nobody there—nobody but Jake.

"I've got some papers to read, Jake." Mr. Gilliard stated. "I'm going to go down to my office. That way you can take your time—and I can get some work done."

"Hey, Jake," Trevor Caldwell picked up the term paper that was lying on the sofa. "Don't let him forget this one." Trevor threw the paper at Jake. "It's Casey's. You know, *Casey*—the one you like so much . . . the one you think is so sweet. And guess what, Jake? That's exactly what Mr. Gilliard thinks. And you know it . . . don't you? You know that Mr. Gilliard just loves Casey. And you better do something about it, Jake. Otherwise, you're just gonna have to lose her . . . just like the other one, huh, Jake? But you know what? You shouldn't worry about it. After all, she's just a little tramp."

"I'll kill you, you ignorant little worm! I'll kill you again!" Jake woke himself up, screaming.

He had to put a stop to this—he had to find a way to get a peaceful night's sleep.

CHAPTER · 29

Chip didn't show up for class on Monday. Or Tuesday. With each passing day, Casey was becoming more and more concerned. She was afraid that Mr. Gilliard might have done exactly what Chip had said he would do. Yet she just couldn't believe that Mr. Gilliard was capable of having Chip expelled.

By Wednesday Casey was determined to find out. She wasn't quite sure how she was going to broach the subject without betraying Chip's confidence. After all, there was still the possibility, however remote, that Mr. Gilliard hadn't read Chip's paper. And she did not want to be the one to call his attention to it.

She stayed in her seat after class, collecting her thoughts, trying to decide how to engage Mr. Gilliard in conversation about Chip.

As the other students ambled out of the room and Mr. Gilliard packed up his briefcase, Slater slid into the seat beside Casey. Chip's place.

"Casey, have you got a minute?"

She didn't. But she was afraid that if she told him that, it would scare him off, and she might never hear what he had to say. "Sure."

"You still want to go to the dance on Saturday?"

"Of course I do." She couldn't believe that someone as awesome as Slater could be so utterly insecure. Margo was right. It *was* kind of adorable.

"Well, I was wondering . . ."

"Yes?" she prodded.

"Would you like to go into town and get something to eat first?"

Before she could answer, they were interrupted by Mr. Gilliard. "Slater, excuse me," he said, coming between them. "I need to have a word with Casey. Privately. If you don't mind."

Slater was unnerved, or maybe upset. Casey couldn't tell. He had a strange look on his face. After an uncomfortable moment, a real stand-off between Slater and Mr. Gilliard, Casey felt that the burden was on her to cut the tension.

"I'll talk to you later," she said, encouraging Slater's departure. As he got up, looking a little dejected, she quickly added, "But yes, I'd like to go."

Slater turned to her and smiled. "Good," he said, and he headed out without a word to Mr. Gilliard.

Mr. Gilliard watched him go, waiting until Slater was out of sight before he began talking.

"Casey, have you seen or heard from Chip this week?" He sat down in the seat Slater had vacated.

"No, I haven't," she answered. "Why do you ask? Is something wrong?"

"I don't know," Mr. Gilliard answered. "I certainly hope not. But he seems to have disappeared."

"You don't know where he went?" Casey was perplexed. Obviously Mr. Gilliard hadn't had Chip expelled: something else was going on. And Mr. Gilliard didn't seem to know any more about it than she did.

"He signed himself out for the weekend, and he hasn't come back. I know the two of you are friends. So I thought maybe you would have some idea where he went."

"Home?" Casey knew that was a ridiculous suggestion. Home was the last place Chip would go—especially if he had a problem. He and Trevor used to take off on a weekend occasionally, sometimes missing a few days of school in the bargain. But Casey didn't know where they went, and she suspected that wherever it was, Chip couldn't afford to go on his own.

"He didn't go home," Mr. Gilliard confirmed what Casey already knew. "The Headmaster called his parents on Monday, and they hadn't heard from him at all. I've been asking all his friends in Bowdin House. Nobody seems to have a clue where he could be."

"So what now?"

"Well, the Headmaster has filed a missing persons report. I guess all we can do is wait."

"You don't think anything bad has happened to him?" It was the first time this awful thought had occurred to Casey. She resolutely pushed it aside. Anyway, no one knew better than Casey how good Chip was at looking out for himself. Well, Casey didn't know where he was and she *was* worried, but no, she didn't think anything bad had happened.

"I tend to doubt it."

So Mr. Gilliard didn't think anything bad had happened, either. Still, he looked and sounded troubled. Casey had to wonder whether Mr. Gilliard had confronted Chip about the term paper, prompting Chip to take off. She couldn't begin to phrase the question.

As it turned out, she didn't have to.

"Casey, may I talk to you in strictest confidence?"

She nodded, a little apprehensively.

"My guess is that if Chip decides to get in touch with anybody here at the school, it's going to be you. And I think it might help if you knew the situation that he's in right now."

Again she nodded, unwilling to volunteer that she already knew the trouble Chip was in. She could listen to Mr. Gilliard say it and discuss it then. But she had given Chip her word, and she wouldn't break it.

"Chip handed in a term paper that he did not write. He bought it." He paused to punctuate the seriousness of the situation.

"Has he been expelled?" Casey tried very hard not to hate Mr. Gilliard. She told herself that he was only doing what he had to do. The rules were clear. Mr. Gilliard wasn't the one who'd made them. And he wasn't the one who'd broken them, either.

But the surprise was that he *had* broken them. "No. He hasn't been expelled. Because I haven't reported it."

Casey was grateful, and she couldn't stop her face from showing it.

"And I'd like to avoid having to do that, if at all possible," he continued. "But I'm going to need Chip's cooperation. That's why I decided to talk to you. If you see him or hear from him, tell him that I am willing to work this out. He's going to pay a very steep price for what he's done. But I will not ruin his chances of being accepted at a good college."

"I'll tell him, Mr. Gilliard. If I hear from him."

Mr. Gilliard reached into his jacket pocket and pulled out a bottle of aspirin. "I just hope it's soon. For his sake as well as mine." He popped some aspirin into his mouth and swallowed them dry.

"You better go now, or you'll be late for your next class."

Casey got up and got her things together. Mr. Gilliard just sat there rubbing his forehead. She wished she could say something smart or comforting to him. He was breaking the rules for one of his students—again—and obviously it troubled him deeply. She hesitated at the door, thinking that maybe she should tell him that he was doing the right thing and that he was a wonderful teacher. But she decided that it would be better if she just left him alone.

CHAPTER · 30

The phone in the hallway on the third floor of Bowdin House rang . . . and rang . . . and rang.

"Everybody in this house must be deaf," Jake said as he made his way up the stairs from the second floor. "Deaf—and blind." Jake was tired. And irritable. It had been weeks since he'd gotten any real sleep—sleep that provided him with any kind of peace, anyway. "Ignorant. That's what they all are, just plain ignorant. Nobody ever hears a thing around here. Old Jake's just gotta take care of everything."

By the time he reached the landing on the third floor, the phone had stopped ringing, and Jake saw Slater standing at the end of the hallway with the receiver in his hand.

Slater saw Jake and smiled. "It's okay, Jake. I've got it."

"You're the only good boy in this house, Sammy," Jake said as he came down the hallway. "The only one."

"Hang on one second, okay?" Slater said into the receiver.

"You know, Sammy, you don't have to always be taking messages for those little worms on this floor," Jake continued. "They got ears, they all got two hands, they can answer the phone once in a while, too, you know."

"It's okay, Jake. It's for me."

"Oh," Jake said. He leaned against the wall near the phone, as if the call were for him, too. "I bet that's your pops again, ain't it? That man sure does love you a lot, Sammy, the way he's been callin' you all the way from overseas."

"Yeah, Jake, he sure does." Slater smiled. "But actually, it's not my father, it's my brother."

"Well, I'll be." Jake leaned in closer to Slater. "Hello there, Adam Laurence," Jake said, loud enough so Adam could hear him on the other end.

Slater laughed, as did Adam on the other end of the line. "Adam says hello," Slater told Jake.

"You make sure you give that boy my best before you hang up that phone." Jake reached into his pocket for his keys. "While I'm up here, I might as well see what kind of shape that Eddie Brewster left his room in—I know he had some kind of party up here last night."

With that, Jake headed for Eddie Brewster's room, only two doors down from the phone.

"Sorry about that, Adam," Slater said into the receiver. "I didn't mean to keep you hanging."

"Don't worry about it," Adam laughed.

"So what's up?"

"Well, believe it or not, Mom and Dad are flying in tonight. Dad didn't call you because they just decided this morning, and he knew you'd be in class."

"You're kidding. I thought they were staying until Monday."

"Well, they were supposed to. But Dad decided to cancel the rest of his meetings so they could get back here for the weekend. They want to take us all out Saturday night so we can celebrate, you know, me and Beth being pregnant. Mom and Dad are gonna stay at a hotel in the city, and I figured you could take the train out Friday afternoon and spend the whole weekend at our place."

Slater was silent. He didn't know what to say. He wanted to have dinner with his family, wanted to celebrate the fact that Adam was going to be a dad—that he was going to be an uncle. But not *this* weekend—not Saturday night—not the night he was finally going to get Casey McCabe all to himself.

Adam reacted to the silence. "What's up?"

"Nothing," Slater lied.

"Something," Adam knew his brother too well to let him off the hook. "Is this not a good weekend for you?"

"Well . . . can we maybe do it next weekend?" Slater's hopes rose.

"No. Mom and Dad have to be in London, remember?"

Again, Slater was silent.

"Do you not want to come out this weekend? Because if you don't, it's okay." Adam was sincere.

"No. It's not that. I want to come—I really do." Slater meant it. "It's just that Saturday night is that stupid dance—you know—the Mischief Night thing."

Slater didn't have to say another word for Adam to know what the problem was. "So who's the lucky girl?"

Slater was grateful his brother understood. "Casey . . . Casey McCabe. She's really nice."

"Isn't she the one you couldn't take your eyes—or your camera—off of on Parents' Day?"

Slater laughed. "Yeah, that was her."

"Why don't you ever learn to listen to your older brother?" Adam kidded. "I told you she'd say yes. So when did you ask her?"

"The other day. And I've got to tell you, I was so nervous, I thought I was going to throw up. I thought for sure she was gonna laugh in my face or something . . . and I'd end up standing there like a fool . . . totally humiliated."

Adam laughed. "That's exactly the way I felt the

first time I asked Beth out. Trust me, the next time will be a lot easier."

"I hope so." Slater wasn't so sure there would be a next time—wasn't even sure he could make it through the first time without something terrible happening. "So what should I do?" Slater asked his brother.

"Well I'll tell you what you're *not* going to do. You're not going to miss a date with the prettiest girl on campus, that's for sure."

Slater was relieved.

"I'll tell you what. Why don't we just have dinner on Friday night? I'm sure it will be fine with Mom and Dad. That way, you can get back to Huntington Saturday afternoon, in plenty of time for the dance."

"That would really be great. Are you sure nobody'll mind?"

"Are you kidding me? When Mom finds out you have a date, she'll be so excited she'll probably start planning a wedding."

Slater laughed.

"Listen, I'll call you later so we can decide what train you need to catch."

"Great." Slater was just about to hang up when he saw Jake come out of Eddie Brewster's room. "Hey, Adam," he caught Adam before Adam hung up. "Jake sends his best," Slater said loudly. He wanted to make sure Jake heard. And he smiled at Jake as he hung up the phone.

But Jake didn't smile back. In fact, Jake looked pretty upset. "So you're goin' to the dance, are you, Sammy?"

Slater realized that he didn't really have to speak loudly for Jake to hear every word. Jake knew exactly what was going on. And Slater was a bit taken aback, not only by the fact that Jake must have been listening to his entire conversation, but by the way Jake was looking at him . . . staring at him. And his tone was different . . . weird . . . unnerving. "Yeah, Jake," Slater managed to answer. "I'm going."

Jake was visibly agitated. "You're makin' a big mistake, Sammy. A big mistake."

"How is that, Jake? How is going to the dance a big mistake?" Slater was more curious than concerned.

"You just listen to me, Sammy. Old Jake knows what he's talkin' about. You just go home and stay home . . . you hear me? I don't want you comin' around here on Mischief Night, you understand?"

"No, Jake. I *don't* understand."

"How many times I got to tell you, Sammy? How many times?"

"Tell me what, Jake? How many times do you have to tell me *what*?" Slater was beginning to wonder whether or not Jake even knew what he was saying. Or who he was talking to, for that matter. For the past few weeks, Jake hadn't quite been himself, not even with Slater. And Slater couldn't help thinking that maybe Jake's drinking was starting to take a toll on him . . . starting to affect his ability to function . . . starting to affect his ability to reason.

"You just stay away from that girl, you hear me, Sammy?" Jake warned.

"Casey?" Slater didn't really have to ask to know that Casey was definitely the girl Jake was referring to. But what on earth did he mean?

"Don't you play the fool with me, boy." Jake was becoming more and more upset. "You know better than that. Old Jake knows better than that."

Slater had never seen Jake so upset. Never. "Jake, I thought you wanted me to look out for Casey. Remember?"

"Yeah, Sammy, I remember." Jake was stuggling with his own thoughts. "That's exactly right. That's exactly what I want you to do . . . look out for that girl . . . that's what I told you." Jake tried to calm himself down.

"Well, that's what I'm doing, Jake. Just what you told me to do. I'm just looking out for her." Slater tried to appease him. "I'm just going to take her to the dance, that's all."

"That's right," Jake tried to appease himself. "It's

just a dance, that's all . . . nothin' to worry about . . . just a dance. That's all it is, right?"

"Yeah, Jake," Slater said as he patted Jake on the back the way Jake always patted him. "Honest. That's all it is."

"Okay, Sammy . . . okay."

♠ ♠ ♠

But it was a lie . . . and they both knew it. It wasn't going to be "just a dance" . . . not for either one of them.

CHAPTER · 31

"Just a few more days." Iggy Boy was in his secret place, talking to the pictures of Casey on the wall above his bed. "And you and I will be together."

Iggy Boy ran his fingers across his favorite picture of Casey . . . the one he'd taken on Parents' Day. "You're so beautiful. So special. Not at all like the other one. Iggy Boy made a mistake with the other one. But Iggy Boy doesn't make the same mistake twice. Does he?"

Iggy Boy took the picture of Casey off the wall and turned it around so that it was facing the pictures of "the other one" . . . the one that was "a mistake." "Look at her, Casey. Look at how beautiful she was." Iggy Boy walked over to the wall. "See?" Iggy Boy held the picture of Casey up close to the wall, as if the picture itself had eyes that could see. "Just like you. And you know what? Iggy Boy wanted her. Almost as badly as Iggy Boy wants you." Iggy Boy shook his head in disgust. "And look at what she made Iggy Boy do." He moved Casey's picture slowly across the wall . . . in front of the row of pictures that clearly documented what Iggy Boy had done. "But Iggy Boy doesn't have to worry about you, does he, Casey? Because you're not like her, are you, Casey?" Iggy Boy turned Casey's picture around so that it was facing him. "You're different, aren't you, Casey?" Iggy Boy stroked Casey's picture again. "Iggy Boy knows you are. And you would never do anything to hurt Iggy Boy . . . to humiliate Iggy Boy . . . now, would you?"

Iggy Boy noticed the picture of Chip Cimino lying on his desk. He'd only taken one. Photographing Chip provided Iggy Boy with no entertainment at all. In fact, had he not wanted to be sensitive to Casey's feelings, he wouldn't even have bothered. A waste of film. But Iggy Boy knew that Casey was fond of Chip . . . not in a bad way . . . not in a way that caused Iggy Boy any worry. So he wanted to give Casey something nice to remember Chip by.

Iggy Boy had kind of liked Chip himself. He'd understood Chip—felt sorry for Chip. While Iggy Boy didn't always approve of Chip's behavior, he could forgive it. After all, Chip Cimino was just trying to fit in . . . just trying to make himself a part of it all . . . just trying to be accepted. And Iggy Boy understood just how difficult that was, at least at

Huntington Prep. "I'm sorry about Chip, Casey. I truly am." Iggy Boy was sincere. "But look how nice he looks."

Iggy Boy picked up the picture of Chip. And it *was* nice . . . at least, as nice as a picture of a dead person could be. Iggy Boy had even covered the bottom half of Chip's body with a blanket, just the way they cover bodies laid out in coffins. He'd even folded Chip's arms across his chest . . . and closed his eyes, they way they did at funeral homes. And Iggy Boy had gone to a whole lot of trouble to comb Chip's hair neatly and wipe the blood from Chip's face so that the camera wouldn't pick it up. Yeah, Iggy Boy had wanted to make sure that Casey had a nice shot of Chip Cimino, lying faceup.

But that's not how Chip Cimino had gone down. In fact, Iggy Boy had hit Chip so hard in the back of the head that Chip's face was the first thing to hit the floor. It was all kind of sad, really. But what was Iggy Boy to do? Chip Cimino was in the wrong place at the wrong time, and Iggy Boy had no choice. It was all Michael Gilliard's fault . . . all of it. Eventually, Casey would understand that. "He didn't feel a thing," Iggy Boy assured the picture of Casey as he laid it down on the desk next to Chip's. "Didn't even know what hit him."

Iggy Boy's attention was immediately focused on Mr. Gilliard. "But that's definitely not going to be the case for you, now is it . . . Mr. Gilliard . . . sir," Iggy Boy said mockingly as he stood directly in front of the only picture he had of Mr. Gilliard . . . the one that looked so ridiculous . . . the one that truly captured what a fool he was. "No. Iggy Boy's gonna make sure you know exactly what's going on . . . exactly what's hit you. I hate to tell you this, pal . . . but there's no way I'm gonna let you stand between Casey and me, ever again. No way at all. So if I were you . . . I'd try and enjoy the dance . . . because it'll be the last one you ever get to attend."

Iggy Boy laughed. Michael Gilliard was definitely in for a very rude awakening . . . and he wasn't the only one.

CHAPTER · 32

At nine-thirty Saturday morning, Slater was already feeling anxious about the dance . . . and a little embarrassed that both Adam and Beth knew it. In fact, Slater's nerves had been the topic of their entire conversation at breakfast—which Slater could barely get down, because his stomach was already beginning to tie itself in a thousand little knots.

Beth thought it was "cute." And Adam was more than empathetic. In fact, they both spent better than an hour trying to assure Slater that the dance would be "just fine," that he would be "just fine." But the dance was more than ten hours away, and Slater was already feeling anything but "just fine."

"I'm telling you," Beth had tried to convince him, "the minute she gets to know you, the minute she gets to see you for who you really are, she's gonna fall madly, passionately in love with you. The same way I fell madly, passionately in love with your brother."

Slater hoped his sister-in-law was right. Only he

couldn't help thinking about how terrible it would be if she wasn't. What if he choked? What if he couldn't even manage to carry on a conversation with Casey? Or even worse. What if he did open up? What if he did let her see him for who he really was? What if she didn't want him then? Maybe Jake was right. Maybe Slater was making a very big mistake.

Slater looked at his watch for the fifteenth time in the same number of minutes. His train didn't leave until noon. And it only took about ten minutes to get to the station from Adam's house. He had to calm down. He had a long way to go before the night even started. And at the rate he was going, he was sure to make it a disaster.

As Slater waited for his brother to shower and dress, he decided to scan the bookcases in Adam's den to look for something to occupy his mind on the train ride back to school. As if that were at all possible. But as he made his way down the shelves, Adam's old Huntington Prep yearbooks caught his eye. He pulled all four of them off the shelf and sat down on the couch to look through them.

He started in chronological order, with Adam's freshman yearbook. And as he flipped through the pages, he couldn't help noticing that Huntington Prep hadn't changed at all. It had looked the same back then as it did now. In fact, except for the hairstyles and the clothing, Adam's freshman yearbook could very well have been Slater's. He even recognized a majority of the faculty members, all of whom—with the exception of Spegman—were still teaching. Even the kitchen staff looked the same. And the maintenance staff, including Jake.

Slater turned to the section of "house pictures" to look for Adam. It was a Huntington Prep tradition for all the residents of each house to be photographed in front of their respective houses as a group—a "family"—at least that's the way the pictures were always labeled. Because Bowdin House was the most prestigious dormitory on campus, it was always the first picture in the section. Year after year, the shot was taken the same way; all the house members grouped together on the stairs, seniors on top, freshmen on the bottom; house maintenance wherever they managed to fit in; and the House Master centered on the porch above them all.

By the time Adam walked into the den, Slater was already working his way through Adam's junior-year yearbook. And he was again looking at "the Bowdin House family" shot.

"Geez. Oh, man," Adam said as he looked over Slater's shoulder. "I can't believe how goofy-looking I was."

"Was?" Slater couldn't resist.

"Yeah," Adam smacked Slater in the back of the head, playfully. "Was."

"Yeah, well if you really want to see goofy, you should take a look at your freshman picture." Slater laughed.

"Oh, come on," Adam shot back. "All freshman are goofy-looking. I mean, look at these guys." Adam pointed to the first row of freshmen in the picture. "Look at how pathetic they all look."

As Slater scanned the lineup, one of the freshmen caught his attention. The last one in the row, the one standing directly in front of Jake. The one who seemed to be trying to turn away from the camera. Only Jake's hands were gripping his shoulders, as if Jake were trying to hold him in place. Even though the picture was taken in black and white, Slater could clearly see that the kid's face was all black and blue. And his eyes were all swollen, swollen so badly that they were practically shut. As Slater studied the face, he couldn't help feeling that there was something familiar about it. He couldn't help thinking that it was someone he knew, only he just couldn't place him. "'Pathetic' doesn't even begin to describe the way this one looks." Slater pointed out the face to Adam.

"Oh, man." Adam's reaction was immediate and sincere. "I always felt so sorry for that kid."

"Who was he?" Slater asked, really wanting to know.

"Nicky. Nicky something. I don't remember his last name."

In all the Huntington Prep yearbooks students' names were listed only under class pictures and team sports, not under "House" pictures or candid shots. Slater was pretty sure that Nicky whatever-his-name-was was not on the football team, so he turned immediately to the freshman class pictures to see if he could find him. "You sure he was a freshman?" Slater asked as he scanned the freshman class pictures.

"Yeah. Why?"

" 'Cause he's not in here."

Adam leaned over Slater's shoulder and scanned the freshman names and faces. "That's weird. Maybe he was sick or something the day they took the shot. I'll tell you what, though," Adam continued, "that poor kid really had a hard time of it. At least at Bowdin House. Apparently he was on some sort of scholarship, and Spenguin hated the fact that he was living in Bowdin House. And there were a bunch of seniors—you know, Spenguin groupies—that were always beating up on him, always doing something to try to humiliate the kid in front of everyone else. The worst part about it was, Spenguin used to allow it, encourage it even. It was like he got a kick out of making the kid's life unbearable." Adam took the yearbook from Slater and flipped to the back, where all the "candid shots" of student life were. "In fact, this was the year that everybody on the yearbook committee got suspended for a week."

Slater looked at Adam curiously. He had no idea where Adam's train of thought was leading, but he figured he might as well go along for the ride. "How come?"

"Because of this." Adam held the yearbook out, pointing to the picture he wanted Slater to see.

Slater couldn't believe the shot. It had been taken in the shower room—the one that used to be on the fourth floor. And it was the same kid . . . sitting on the floor, with his hands tied around the shower pipes, looking all bruised and beaten. He was wearing only a towel, and there was a toilet-paper banner wrapped around his chest, like a banner on a beauty pageant contestant. On the banner were written the words "spit ball."

"I can't believe they actually got this picture through," Slater said as he shook his head in disgust. "Weren't there any yearbook advisors?"

"Not back then. But I'll tell you what: the year after this happened, they made sure they put together an entire committee."

"Tell me about it," Slater groaned. He knew all too well the red tape involved in putting together the yearbook these days.

Adam flipped through the pages. "The only thing that topped the hysteria that picture produced was Cameron Wheeler's suicide."

"Who was Cameron Wheeler?"

"The kid who took the picture. Jake found him hanging in the maintenance closet a few weeks after the yearbook came out."

Slater felt a chill run up his spine. "He killed himself? You're kidding me."

"No. He was in all kinds of trouble with the school. And his parents. I guess he just snapped. I really didn't know him all that well, didn't really want to. He was the kind of kid only Spenguin could appreciate. You know what I mean?"

Slater nodded. He knew exactly what Adam meant. And he couldn't help thinking about Trevor Caldwell. Trevor Caldwell, who'd been found hanging at the end of Jake's vacuum cord. "And what about Jake?" Slater's mind was starting to move in a direction he didn't like at all.

"What *about* Jake?" Adam looked confused.

"Did he have anything to do with Cameron Wheeler?"

"No. Jake hated Cameron Wheeler." Adam answered innocently, unaware of the question's intent. "In fact, Cameron Wheeler used to cause Jake all kinds of heartache. I mean, I'm sorry he died but like I told you, he was a real little scum."

Slater realized that his brother had no idea where he was heading and figured he would leave it that way, at least for the moment. "And what about that kid, Nicky? How was Jake with him?" Slater posed the questions as innocuously as he possibly could.

"I guess he liked him. At least, that's the impression I always got. Why? What's the sudden obsession with Jake's take on the situation?" Adam continued flipping through the pages.

"I don't know," Slater lied. "I was just asking. That's all."

"Yeah, well, this is the kid Jake *really* liked," Adam was lost in his own reminiscences. "Sammy Carson. Check it out." Adam showed Slater the page. "Sammy even took his senior picture with Jake. Hey, isn't Jake always calling you Sammy?"

"Yeah," Slater answered.

"I'll bet that's why," Adam speculated. "The two of you look kind of alike," Adam continued. "You should actually be flattered. Sammy Carson was one of the nicest guys at Huntington Prep."

"Did he live in Bowdin House?" Slater almost didn't want to know.

"Uh-huh. He was a year ahead of me. Poor Jake. He was devastated when Sammy died."

Slater's heart was starting to race. "Sammy *died*?"

"Yeah. Not too long after Cameron Wheeler. It was really sad."

"Don't tell me they found him hanging in the maintenance closet, too." Slater was almost too afraid to hear what had happened to Sammy.

Adam laughed at the way Slater said it. "No. Sammy drowned. It was an accident."

"At Huntington?" Slater couldn't hide his increasing trepidation. "Who found him? Jake?"

"No. One of the guys who worked in the field house. What the heck is the matter with you?" Adam suddenly reacted to the look on Slater's face, the tone of his questions.

"And didn't you have a kid in your class who disappeared or something? You know, the one whose parents were on that talk show?" Slater's mind was racing.

"A class ahead of me," Adam said hesitantly. "His name was Justin Taylor. Nobody really knows what happened to him."

"Maybe somebody ought to try asking Jake."

Adam laughed. "What's that supposed to mean?"

"Think about it, Adam. You heard Jake on Parents' Day. Don't you remember?" Slater did his best Jake impersonation. "Between you and me and that lamppost over there, Spenguin's death weren't no accident."

Adam rolled his eyes. "Slater, you're talking about Jake. He always goes on like that. It doesn't mean anything."

"And what about Trevor Caldwell, huh?" Slater wasn't about to quit. "Spenguin adored him, just like he adored Cameron Wheeler, and he ends up hanging by a vacuum cord. And now this guy Chip Cimino is missing . . . for, like, a week . . . what about that? Huh? What do you think about that?"

"I think you're panicking over your date with Casey. And your nerves are just trying to find a brand-new outlet."

"I'm serious." Slater was.

"Slater, get a grip on yourself, will you?" Adam turned back to the Bowdin House picture. "You see this guy?" He pointed to a picture. "He treated Jake a whole lot worse than Cameron Wheeler ever did. And you know where he is now? In Aspen. With a wife and three kids. And this guy," Adam pointed to another picture. "Jake hated him with a passion, used to tell me all the time how much he wanted to wring his neck. But he didn't. I know for sure because he's living right down the street from me. And you see this guy," again Adam pointed. "Okay," Adam hesitated. "Well, *he's* dead."

Slater's eyes widened.

"But it was a car accident. In Stockholm, I think. And as far as I know, Jake is not a world traveler."

Slater laughed, first at Adam, and then at himself. "I guess you're right."

"Of course I'm right."

"It's just that Jake really weirded me out the other day. You know he listened to our entire phone conversation?"

"What's so weird about that? Jake's been listening to other people's conversations since I lived in Bowdin House."

"Yeah, I know. But he was really upset. He told me I was making a real big mistake by going to the dance."

"I'll tell you what," Adam looked at his watch. "If we don't get a move on it, you *are* gonna make a really big mistake—by missing the train."

As Slater stepped onto the train, Adam Laurence remembered Nicky's last name. "Gilliard," he said aloud. Only Slater didn't hear him. He had already disappeared onto the train. And as the doors of the train started to close, Adam's mind flashed back to Parents' Day . . . back to the very moment he shook "Mickey" Gilliard's hand.

CHAPTER · 33

Jake heard the screams coming from the fourth-floor shower room . . . the screams . . . and the laughter. And as he made his way down the hallway, he saw them . . . all the trash . . . gathered outside the bathroom door, as if there were some kind of show going on inside. "What's goin' on in there?" Jake shoved his way through the filth. "What are you ignoramuses up to now?"

The moment Jake reached the door . . . saw what was going on . . . he wanted to kill them all . . . for what they'd done, for what they were doing. Only he just stood there, scared out of his mind . . . scared by what was happening to the boy, petrified . . . by the sight of Mr. Spegman . . . who was just standing there, right inside the doorway, takin' in the show . . . and chuckling like he was watchin' a cartoon or somethin'.

"Dear Lord." Jake should never have let the words escape . . . at least not with a tone like that . . . a tone that was pained and repulsed. No . . . if Jake was gonna say anything at all . . . it should have been with a smile on his face, with laughter in his voice . . . and then no one would have noticed, and Mr. Spegman would never have known he was there.

And suddenly . . . it was as if all eyes were on Jake . . . including the boy's . . . and Jake couldn't pull himself away, away from those eyes, the boy's eyes . . . the ones that were so tormented . . . so full of pain . . . and they were pleading with Jake, pleading for help . . . only Jake couldn't move . . . and Jake couldn't scream. And for one split second . . . Jake was sure he saw his granddaddy looking back at him through that boy's eyes.

"Jake," the sound of Mr. Spegman's voice immediately focused Jake's attention. "Your presence is not required here," Mr. Spegman spoke calmly. "As you can see, everything here is quite under control." No question, Mr. Spegman was a pro, really knew how to work his audience. "Which is not the case in the laundry room, now is it, Jake?"

Everyone laughed . . . at Jake . . . at how easy it was for Spenguin to humiliate him.

"Is it, Jake?" Mr. Spegman wanted an answer . . . wanted to make sure Jake stepped back into place.

And before Jake could answer . . . he wasn't there anymore, he was in the field house . . . watching Mr. Spegman topple down the stairs. Only the stairs seemed endless . . . seemed to go on forever . . . not like the ones that Mr. Spegman really fell down . . . and Jake was sure that he was watching Spenguin falling all the way to hell. "Did you think Iggy Boy would forget about you?" Jake screamed at Mr. Spegman as he continued falling. "Did you? You can't treat people like that, Mr. Spegman, sir . . . can't treat people like that at all without expecting bad things to happen."

"Jake." The voice startled Jake . . . and Spenguin suddenly disappeared. "Is that you?" The voice echoed from somewhere in the distance.

"Sammy?" Jake looked around the empty field house from where he was standing. "Sammy, where are you, boy?"

"Right where you left me, Jake," the voice answered. "You know where I am."

Jake's heart started pounding . . . and before he knew it the halls in the field house seemed to be moving . . . toward him . . . past him . . . and suddenly he was standing directly in front of the door that opened up into the pool room. The pool where all the swimming meets were held. And before Jake knew it . . . he was gripping the handle . . .

"Come on in, Jake," the voice beckoned.

"Please, Sammy," Jake's tone reflected the pain he was feeling. "Please don't make me do this again."

"Do what, Jake? You didn't do anything."

That was the truth . . . only Jake couldn't face it . . . couldn't live with it . . . couldn't ever seem to get away from it.

"I know that," the voice continued. "We know that."

Jake's heart stopped. She was in there . . . with Sammy . . . that pretty little girl . . . the one Jake liked so much . . . the one Sammy just couldn't stay away from. "Please, Sammy," Jake pleaded. "Please don't make me go through this again." Jake started to tremble.

The door seemed to open by itself . . . and Jake had no choice but to look . . . at what Iggy Boy had done.

CHAPTER · 34

Casey fell hard and fast. And she never knew what hit her, never saw it coming.

Nothing like this had ever happened to Casey before. She didn't even believe it was possible. It was like love at first sight. Only it wasn't first sight at all. She'd known Slater for nearly four years. But suddenly it felt as though she'd only just met him for the first time. And at the same time, it felt as though she'd known him all her life. It was a curious feeling: brand-new, and yet familiar, comfortable, and safe.

They talked for two solid hours about everything and nothing, barely touching the pizza they'd ordered.

Slater confessed that he'd been interested in Casey from the moment he'd first laid eyes on her. He even remembered what she was wearing and how she had her hair pulled back, and where she sat first homeroom period, freshman year. He told her how, at the first freshman dance, he'd stood in a dark corner watching her across the room, too afraid to approach her.

Casey remembered that dance, too. She remembered standing there, all alone, new at the school, not having had time to make any friends yet, just praying that someone would ask her to dance. But nobody had. Even the goofy guys had just walked around her, as if she wasn't even there. She'd left that dance in tears. By the time she'd gotten her father on the phone, she was sobbing. Her father had told her that he wasn't surprised that nobody had asked her to dance, because boys never asked the prettiest girl in the room to dance. They were too afraid of being shot down. And even though she hadn't believed it, it had comforted her to hear her father tell her that her problem was that she was too pretty. Of course he'd thought that; he was her father. Even father lizards thought their kids were pretty.

Slater laughed when she said that. She liked making him laugh. And she liked the way his eyes sparkled when he did. And she liked the way he looked at her — looked her right in the eye — when he told her that her father was right. He hadn't asked her to dance because he couldn't imagine someone as beautiful and smart and wonderful as she was being interested in him.

And then he made her laugh when he told her

that the other reason he hadn't asked her to dance was because whenever he tried to dance, somebody always ended up calling 911.

But that was silly. Slater was a wonderful dancer. She loved the way he held her, his right arm wrapped around her, hand resting on the small of her back, his left hand holding her right against his chest, over his heart. And Casey felt as though the two of them were moving as if they were one.

Not at all like poor Margo, who had Eddie Brewster trampling all over her feet, with David Cross waiting on the sidelines for his turn.

As Margo and Eddie moved past Casey and Slater, Margo winked at Casey and mouthed the words, "I told you so." Then she punched Eddie again, practically screaming at him, "Get off my feet, you baboon."

Slater laughed. "Poor Margo," he whispered in Casey's ear. "She could have come with us, you know." Slater knew all about Margo and why she was there with Eddie and David. It was one of the many things Casey had confessed to him over pizza.

"Well, at least she's getting the show she came to see," Casey said.

Casey couldn't believe it. It felt so right to be in Slater's arms, looking into his eyes. She wondered how she'd ever thought of those eyes as cold and distant and unreadable. His eyes weren't that way at all, not the way he looked at her now. His eyes were soft and gentle, and she knew exactly what they were telling her. He wanted to kiss her. He was going to kiss her. And she lifted her face, inviting it. Her eyes closed as his lips touched hers, and he pulled her closer against him. It was a perfect kiss; neither awkward nor urgent, but a kiss between two people who have known one another forever. When it was over, he looked into her eyes again and smiled contentedly, and they went on dancing.

And Casey smiled, too, as she rested her head on Slater's shoulder.

It was so intimate a moment that Casey almost forgot that they were not alone. Only slowly did she become aware again of the other people in the room. And it wasn't until she noticed Margo staring at them with a satisfied smile on her face that Casey realized, with a twinge of embarrassment, that any number of people could have been watching that kiss. Just as that thought occurred to her, she saw Mr. Gilliard looking at them, as well. But as her eyes met his, he turned and headed into the next room.

She began to feel even more embarrassed and self-conscious. It was like getting caught by a parent. And she imagined that that was the look she saw on Mr. Gilliard's face—parental disapproval. She even thought she saw him shake his head, too, the way her father did when he was disappointed.

But Casey caught herself, decided that paranoia was getting the better of her. And she couldn't let that happen. Now was not the time for her to be thinking about Mr. Gilliard, or anyone else—except Slater. She looked into his eyes again, and he returned the gaze. Suddenly it felt as though it was just the two of them again. The only thing that mattered was that she was happy in Slater's arms.

And Casey wasn't the only one who felt that way.

CHAPTER · 35

"Not again, Sammy." Jake felt the pain that tore through his chest and shot straight up to his brain. "You can't do this to old Jake . . . you can't do this again."

Jake couldn't pull his eyes away from Slater dancing with that pretty little girl—the one Jake liked so much, the one Jake told him to stay away from, the one he had no business holding . . . touching . . . kissing.

"I'm just gonna take her to the dance." Slater's words echoed through Jake's head. "Honest. That's all it is."

"You ignorant, ignominious piece of scum," the voice in Jake's head bellowed. "You're the one who allowed this to happen. Aren't you, Jake? Look at yourself. Look at how pathetic you are. Come on, Jake. Do something. Do something about it. Before Iggy Boy does." Jake started trembling. And the voice inside his head started to laugh. "You know what, Jake?" The voice mocked him. "Why don't you just stand here and do nothing? Just the way you always do. Just the way you did with your granddaddy. Huh, Jake? You just stood there. Doing nothing. Knowing exactly what was gonna happen. Didn't you, Jake?"

Jake could feel himself coming apart. He wanted to scream, wanted to grab Slater right then and there, in front of everyone, and put a stop to it all. Only he couldn't, because he knew it was too late.

Jake headed out of the dance, down to the basement. He needed a drink more than he had ever needed one before. And as he took the cap off the bottle of Jack Daniels—hoping to escape, hoping to quiet all the noises in his head—something deep down inside stopped him. It was time for Jake to face the truth. Time for Jake to face himself.

And all at once the voices disappeared . . . all but one.

CHAPTER · 36

Casey had been gone a long time. With every minute—every second—that passed, Slater was growing more and more impatient. He'd had something to drink, something to eat, talked to a few people, all the while waiting and watching for Casey's return.

It was silly. He knew it. He even managed to find himself amusing. Casey would certainly find it amusing that he was feeling like a lovesick puppy, lost without her for even a couple of minutes.

But it was more than a couple of minutes now. And Slater found himself fighting the feeling that something was wrong.

"Where's Casey?" Margo asked, coming up beside Slater. She appeared to have escaped from Eddie and David, but probably not for long.

"I thought maybe she was with you," Slater answered.

"Nope. Haven't seen her in awhile. Don't tell me she ditched you," Margo teased.

"I'm beginning to wonder." There was concern in his voice and Margo picked up on it.

"You can't be serious!" Margo laughed. "She's probably in the bathroom."

"Yeah, that's where she said she was going. But she's been gone an awfully long time."

"Girls take longer."

"Would you go check? Make sure she's all right?"

"Look, Slater, this is really sweet. I mean, I think it's sweet. But you've got to get it under control. Because nothing is gonna turn Casey off faster than if you start acting all possessive. Trust me, I know her."

"I know what you're saying, Margo." He'd been telling himself the same thing for at least twenty minutes now. But he had begun to feel that in his effort to give Casey space, he had been negligent. Because the little voice in the back of his head—the voice that was never wrong—was telling him that Casey was in trouble. "I'm not trying to be possessive. Really. It's just that she's been gone so long, that I'm beginning to think she's sick or something."

"Or maybe there's a line."

"Maybe," he humored Margo and hoped she was right. "But I'd feel a whole lot better if you checked for me."

"The things we do for love," Margo quipped as she headed off to find out about Casey.

"Thanks," Slater said.

Slater turned around and scanned the room in another futile attempt to spot Casey among the crowd. But it wasn't Casey who he saw moving toward him. It was Jake, looking worse than Slater had ever seen him.

Jake was soaking wet and was walking like a zombie toward Slater, bumping into people along the way. People turned to look at him, shook their heads and snickered. But no one paid too much attention. It was only Flakey Jake, after all.

"Sammy," Jake bellowed, loud enough to be heard over the music.

Slater rushed over to him. He didn't want Jake to make a spectacle of himself, or of Slater, for that matter. "What is it, Jake?" Slater made a conscious effort to keep his tone casual, to behave normally, even though the chill than ran through him told him that there was nothing normal about Jake. Not tonight.

"Why didn't you listen to me?" Jake sounded both hopeless and angry at the same time.

"What are you talking about, Jake?"

"Didn't I tell you to stay away from that girl?"

"Casey?"

Jake just hung his head and nodded.

"You told me to look out for her," Slater reminded him.

"Yeah," Jake remembered. "Look out for her. Not be holdin' her, touchin' her, kissin' her," he accused.

Slater realized that they were beginning to attract attention. "Why don't we go outside and talk," he suggested, figuring that a little fresh air would do Jake some good.

"Yeah, we better go. We ain't got much time, you and me." Jake grabbed Slater by the arm and rushed him through the crowd and out the door like a bouncer giving someone the bum's rush.

It was raining outside. Slater hadn't realized that, hadn't heard it over the noise inside. And he was surprised when Jake dragged him off the porch into the rain. When Slater realized that Jake intended to keep going—he didn't know where—he yanked his arm free and stopped in the middle of the path in front of Bowdin House.

"Jake, what's wrong with you?"

"Plenty. That's why you gotta come with me now. To put it right."

Slater wasn't about to go anywhere with Jake. Not the way he was acting. For the first time, Slater was beginning to think that maybe the others were right about Jake, maybe he was certifiably insane. "Go with you where, Jake?"

"You know where we gotta go," Jake said sadly. "To the field house, Sammy. To the pool."

It hit him so hard that Slater actually staggered

backward a few steps. Sammy. Sammy drowned. It was an accident. Or was it? Slater was slowly backing away from Jake. "Why do we have to go to the field house?"

"Because, Sammy, that's where the girl is."

"Casey's not at the field house, Jake. She's inside. At the dance." But even as he said it, even as he tried to make himself believe it, he knew it wasn't true. He knew that Margo was not going to find Casey in the bathroom. Because Casey was at the field house, just as Jake said she was. Something was terribly wrong. What was Casey doing at the field house? And how did Jake know she was there? Then the awful possibility occurred to him that perhaps it was because Jake had taken her there himself.

"No sir, that girl is not inside," Jake assured him. "You know it as well as I do, Sammy. And if you ever want to see her again, you'll come with me, right now." Without another word, Jake turned and started running down the path toward the field house.

There was nothing Slater could do but follow.

CHAPTER · 37

Casey sat huddled in the dark, under the bleachers in the skating rink. She was sopping wet and chilled to the bone. She shivered violently, not so much from the cold as from the thought of Iggy Boy.

He was out there. Waiting for her. Intending to kill her. He'd already tried—tried to drown her in the pool. It was a miracle that she'd gotten away from him.

But she was far from safe. In fact, she was trapped. There was no way out of the field house. All the exterior doors were chained shut. She'd ducked into the skating rink in the desperate hope that the doors that opened to the parking lot would be passable. But they, too, were chained.

The only way out was the way they'd come in, through the maintenance entrance. And Casey knew that she would never make it past Iggy Boy to escape that way. So she barricaded herself in the skating rink by using hockey sticks to jam the door handles. And she hid in the dark.

Several minutes passed. Casey was surprised she didn't hear him moving in the hallway. Surely he had followed her. She wondered why he hadn't even tried the door. Then she imagined that he was just outside, waiting for her. Time was on his side. It was Saturday night. The field house was closed until Monday morning. He had thirty-six hours to take care of her.

But Casey wasn't the only one Iggy Boy was after. Maybe he wasn't waiting outside the doors. Maybe he wasn't even in the field house anymore. Maybe he'd left to go after Slater. That thought nearly drove Casey insane. She couldn't let anything happen to Slater. Yet she didn't dare open the door and risk facing Iggy Boy again.

Iggy Boy was insane, totally and completely insane. There wasn't even a trace of the kind and gentle man she'd thought she knew. He didn't even look the same, didn't even sound the same. But she hadn't noticed that until it was too late, until he'd lured her outside Bowdin House and abducted her.

He'd taken her to the field house, to the pool room, and made her dance with him, just like he'd seen her dance with Sammy. And he'd made her kiss him, just like he'd seen her kiss Sammy. And Casey had complied. Calmly. With a smile on her face. Because by that time she had realized that she was playing for time and quite probably playing for her life.

But Iggy Boy didn't like the kiss. He'd pushed her

away from him. Hard. Casey had fallen backward, toppling over the bleachers and slicing her hand. It was a deep cut, all the way to the bone—the kind of cut that takes awhile to bleed and even longer to hurt. But Iggy Boy had just looked down at her, without concern and without pity. She was a liar, he'd said. She didn't care for him one bit, didn't really want to kiss him. The kiss that she'd given him was nothing like the one she'd shared with Sammy.

Sammy. Casey had known he meant Slater. It was Slater she'd kissed, not Sammy. She didn't even know a Sammy. But he did. And Casey had thought that if she could find out who Sammy was, find out what Sammy had done that was so unforgivable, she could talk to him about it and bring him back to reality.

But when she'd asked about Sammy, he'd flown into a rage. Sammy wasn't the issue. Sammy wasn't even important. Except that Sammy couldn't be allowed to live, not after he'd been holding her, touching her, kissing her.

The only thing that mattered to Iggy Boy was that she had betrayed him, betrayed his love. And Casey had stood there, stunned as a deer in headlights, her gashed hand finally pouring blood, as she listened to Iggy Boy describe in graphic detail his demonstrations of love. He'd told her about Trevor, whose last moment on this earth had been spent regretting what he'd done to Casey. And Chip. An unfortunate circumstance. But

Iggy Boy had gone to all the trouble of burying him properly and respectfully, for Casey's sake.

Casey had tried to hide her revulsion, her shock, her distress. She hadn't wanted to do or say anything to provoke him. But he must have seen it on her face or in her eyes.

"Please don't look at me like that," he'd said. And his voice had sounded normal. There'd been tears in his eyes. And for one brief, hopeful moment Casey had thought she'd reached him. But as quickly as they had appeared, the tears were gone. His eyes had stared vacantly, then flashed to life, cold and malicious once again. They had been Iggy Boy's eyes.

That was when he had lunged at her, told her that she was worse than "the other one." There'd been no place for Casey to run. The only thing she'd been able to think to do was jump into the pool. He'd gone in after her, and there'd been a struggle. But she'd gotten away.

Casey sat in the dark under the bleachers, trying to hold herself together, trying to think of what to do next. Her hand was throbbing and still bleeding. She couldn't just sit there and wait to bleed to death, or freeze to death, or worse.

There had to be a way out. And she was going to have to find it by herself. Because nobody was going to come looking for her—not here. No one knew she was in the field house . . . no one but Iggy Boy.

CHAPTER · 38

Jake entered the field house through the same door Iggy Boy always used . . . the one that didn't lock the right way . . . the one that was so easy to get open. The one that no one ever used . . . no one but the maintenance crew. As Jake stepped inside, he held the door open for Slater, who stopped dead in his tracks.

"What's the matter with you, boy?"

Slater didn't answer. He just stood outside the door, in the pouring rain, looking terrified.

"Now you listen to me, Sammy," Jake commanded. "You can just stand there and do nothin', knowing that if you do that, that pretty little girl doesn't have a prayer in hell. Or you can get that skinny little butt of yours in here and try and do something about it. You understand me?"

Slater's heart was pounding. And as he stood there looking at Jake, he was sure he was seeing someone he didn't know. Even Jake's eyes seemed different to Slater. He'd never seen them so clear, so focused. And Jake's tone was different. Deeper. More controlled. And for the first time, Slater was sure that Jake knew exactly what he was saying. And he understood one thing—Casey was in serious trouble.

"Now are you gonna walk through that door, or am I gonna have to carry you in?" Jake issued the ultimatum.

Slater moved through the doorway into the field house without ever taking his eyes off Jake.

"You just follow me." And with that, Jake headed down the corridor that opened up into the lower level of the field house.

Slater wanted to run. But he didn't. He couldn't. He had to find Casey. And something told him that the only way to do that was to follow Jake. So he did, making sure to keep a safe distance, several paces behind.

The minute Jake reached the stairwell . . . the one that Iggy Boy had thrown Mr. Spegman down . . . the one that led to the upper level on the opposite side of the building from where the pool was located . . . he stopped and turned around to make sure Slater was right behind him. Only he wasn't. Slater was so far behind that Jake was sure he was thinking about trying to take off into the field house by himself to look for Casey. And there was no way Jake was going to allow that to happen, no way at all.

The moment Jake turned around, Slater stopped. He'd been planning to do exactly what Jake thought he might try. Only now it was too late; now, Jake was moving toward him. And before Slater could get away, Jake grabbed him by the shirt.

"Now you listen to me." Jake pulled Slater toward the stairwell forcefully. "And you listen to me real good," Jake's voice dropped to an angry whisper. "Unless you want to find yourself lying dead on this landing, the same way Spenguin found his sorry behind, you'll stay right with me. You got that?"

Slater nodded through the fear as Jake practically pushed him up the first step.

"We're goin' up, Sammy." Jake took the first step. "We're goin' up to get that girl."

The minute Jake reached the upper level, he grabbed Slater by the arm. "She's down there," Jake pointed to the other end of the field house. "Down by the pool." Jake started moving down the hallway. Slowly. Carefully. Dragging Slater right along with him. "Say your prayers, Sammy," Jake said as they came closer to the door that led into the pool room. "Just say your prayers."

The floor in front of the pool room door was soaking wet, as was the rest of the hallway that ended at the stairwell on the other side. And as Slater stood in front of the door, he couldn't help gasping at the sight of blood smeared all over the glass window on the inside of the door.

From behind Jake quickly covered Slater's mouth with his hand. "You just pull yourself together, you hear me?" Jake whispered quietly into Slater's ear. "Otherwise, the game is over. You better just take yourself a deep breath, 'cause we're goin' in there. Okay?"

Slater nodded.

"And no matter what, you keep your eyes open and your mouth shut. Got me?"

Again, Slater nodded. As Jake took his hand away from his mouth, Slater wanted to scream. Only something in his head told him not to. Something in his head told him to listen to Jake.

Jake opened the door slowly, quietly. And he stepped inside. He gestured for Slater to do the same.

Slater couldn't believe his eyes. There was blood all over the stairs between the bleachers, the stairs that led down to the pool. And the cement flooring around the pool looked as though a swim meet had just taken place. Water was everywhere. And there were footprints, wet footprints, all around the pool—footprints that Slater was sure belonged to Casey. Casey. And somebody else.

"She got away, Sammy," Jake told him as his eyes scanned the room. "That pretty little girl got away."

Slater couldn't tear his eyes away from Jake's feet,

from Jake's shoes, the shoes that appeared to be the same size as the prints down by the pool.

"But she's in this building somewhere, Sammy," Jake continued. "Got to be. There's only one way out. And that girl is smart enough to know that there'd be no way to get back through that door. Not without being seen. Come on," Jake grabbed Slater and pulled him out of the pool room. "We gotta find her."

The trail of blood splattering the floor leading to the stairwell and covering the banister leading down the stairs to the first level led Jake and Slater directly to the doors of the skating rink. "This is it, Sammy," Jake said as he reached out for the handle on one of the doors. "The end of the line." Jake pushed the handle to open the door. But the door wouldn't open. "Now I know this door ain't locked." Jake pushed the handle again, harder. The door gave, just a little bit, just enough for Jake to see that it was jammed. "This is one smart little girl, Sammy," Jake said as he tried to look through the crack in the door. "One smart little girl." Jake pulled Slater closer to the door. "Call her."

Slater just stood there looking terrified.

"What's the matter with you, boy? I said call her."

Slater shook his head.

"She'll come to you, Sammy. The minute she hears your voice, she'll come to you. As long as she still can." Jake gripped Slater's arm more firmly. "Now call her. Call her and get her to open this door. 'Cause if you don't, I swear to you, Sammy, I'll bust it down."

Slater didn't have any choice but to do exactly what Jake wanted him to do. "Casey," Slater called through the door. "Casey, it's me. Slater."

Jake was right. The minute Casey heard Slater's voice, she ran for the door. And when she opened it, she saw Iggy Boy.

Chapter · 39

"Say cheese."

Slater turned around, away from the terrified look on Casey's face, toward the terrifying voice that was coming from directly behind him.

The instant Slater turned, a flash went off. And Iggy Boy laughed. "I love these candid shots. Don't you, Sammy?" Iggy Boy snapped another. "I always find them so amusing. Particularly in retrospect." He snapped another. "Oh, I'm sorry," Iggy Boy focused the camera on Casey. "I called him Sammy again, didn't I, sweetheart?" Another flash.

Casey didn't answer. She didn't dare.

"Please forgive me, Slater," Iggy Boy affected a tone of sincerity as he extended his hand.

Slater didn't move.

"It was a foolish mistake," Iggy Boy continued as he let his hand drop down to his side. "Total ignorance on my part." He moved closer to Slater. "And while you do bear an uncanny resemblance, you couldn't possibly be Sammy Carson, for one very good reason." Iggy Boy smiled sardonically as he took his dramatic pause. "You're still breathing."

Slater looked horrified and confused.

"Any you're nowhere near as bloated. Or as blue." Iggy Boy laughed. "Isn't that right, Jake?"

Iggy Boy's voice echoed through the field house and resounded through Jake's head.

"Look at him," Iggy Boy ridiculed. "Look at the way he's staring at me. Like a pathetic little lamb who doesn't even know he's about to be led to the slaughter. What's the matter, Slater? Cat got your tongue?"

Slater didn't answer.

"Must be." Iggy Boy felt his jacket pockets as if he were looking for something. "I know *I* don't," Iggy Boy mocked. "At least, not yet, anyway." Iggy Boy's tone turned very angry. "So speak up, you ignominious piece of scum, while you still have the chance. Come on. Offer up some kind of defense for yourself. It's always my favorite part."

Slater looked to Casey, his eyes pleading for some kind of help, some kind of insight.

"Don't look at her," Iggy Boy bellowed. "She's not going to help you. In fact, she's done quite enough for you already. Haven't you, Casey?"

Casey didn't answer.

"Besides, I already know her side of the story. We've already relived her side of the story. And guess what?" Iggy Boy was becoming more and more agitated. "She's already been convicted. So if I were you, I'd come up with something really good. Something much more imaginative. Something that might sway the hands of justice."

"Please, Mr. Gilliard," Slater's voice conveyed his trepidation. "I'm not sure I understand."

"Mr. Gilliard?" Iggy Boy cracked up. "Please, Mr. Gilliard?" Iggy Boy grabbed Slater and turned him around so that he was holding him from behind, with his arm wrapped tightly around his throat. Then Iggy Boy affected Michael Gilliard's voice. "Please, Mr. Gilliard, what? Hmm? Please, Mr. Gilliard, save me?" Iggy Boy laughed as his voice took on its own characteristics again. "Michael Gilliard couldn't even save himself. Isn't that right, Jake?"

The eyes that haunted Jake were suddenly staring at him, through him, with an intensity that seemed to command submission. Only this time Jake held their gaze. This time, Jake had no intention of turning away. This time, there was only one voice inside his head, the voice he trusted. The voice he finally heard clearly. The voice that never steered him wrong. "Don't do this, Mickey." Jake spoke calmly, clearly, compassionately. "You don't want to hurt that boy."

"Mickey's not here anymore, Jake," Iggy Boy's

voice seemed to waver just a bit. "Mickey died in the shower room. Remember?" Iggy Boy tightened his grip around Slater's throat. "What do you say we all head over to the pool for a little party. I've got plenty of booze." Iggy Boy smiled sardonically at Jake. "How 'bout it, Jake? Couple of drinks and you won't remember seeing a thing."

Iggy Boy's words cut through Jake like a knife.

"Control, Jake," Iggy Boy continued to spew. "It's all about control. Didn't Spenguin teach you anything? For chrissake," Iggy Boy laughed. "I know the Bowdin House boys are stupid, but did you really think that they'd keep hiding expensive bottles of booze in the same place when it always disappeared? Keeping you flying cost me a fortune."

Iggy Boy had delivered the blow in an attempt to level Jake. Only Jake didn't flinch. He just stood there, shaking his head sadly. While Iggy Boy was most certainly cruel, he was not responsible for Jake's actions. No, Jake never blamed anyone for his own behavior. In fact, as far as Jake was concerned, Iggy Boy was right. It was all about control, self-control. And Jake was not about to relinquish his own. Not now. Not ever again. "That's all over with now, Mickey," Jake stayed focused, staring right through Iggy Boy as though he could see right down to his very soul. "It's all over with."

Iggy Boy laughed, clearly taken aback by Jake's

reaction. "Sure it is." The nervousness in Iggy Boy's voice was much more noticeable than the sarcasm.

Jake continued, undaunted. "Jake don't blame you for none of it, Mickey. None of this is your fault."

For a moment, Iggy Boy stood silent, his eyes transfixed. Now it was Iggy Boy who was fighting for some self-control. And Jake knew it. Because now, the eyes looking back at Jake had softened— just a bit—just enough for Jake to know that his words were being heard.

But before Jake could continue, Iggy Boy closed his eyes in an attempt to shield himself, threw back his head almost convulsively, and screamed. "Shut up, Jake! You hear me! You just shut your stupid mouth!"

Slater gasped as Iggy Boy strenghtened his hold.

"Blame me," Iggy Boy laughed uncomfortably. "You ought to thank me, Jake, for being kind enough to keep you out of it. Kind enough to keep you alive. In fact, instead of trying to irritate me, you might want to be smart about this whole thing, Jake, and come with me down to the pool room so that we can drink a toast to your good fortune. That way, we can make this entire little episode more palatable for you, and a whole lot easier for us both."

"There ain't gonna be no toast, Mickey," Jake stood his ground. "And there ain't gonna be no 'little episode' either." Jake took a step closer to Iggy Boy. "Now why don't you be smart about this, Mickey, and let the boy go. 'Cause old Jake knows that you don't really want to hurt nobody."

"You better stay where you are, Jake," Iggy Boy said, vibrating. "'Cause I swear, I'll kill him. I'll kill him right here if you want."

"Now, why would you wanna do that? Huh, Mickey?" Jake took another step. "That boy didn't do anything to hurt you. Sammy never did anything to hurt you."

Iggy Boy laughed, almost nervously. "Oh, come on, Jake. Guilt by association is still guilt. And just as punishable. Justice. What goes around comes around. Isn't that the way it works?"

"Yeah, Mickey," Jake said calmly. "That's the way it works. All by itself. That's the way it works."

"No, Jake." Iggy Boy was trembling. "It doesn't work all by itself. *I* make it work!"

"Look at that girl, Mickey." Jake pointed to Casey. "What kind of justice would be done by hurting her?"

"An eye for an eye, Jake."

"But she didn't hurt you, Mickey. She doesn't even know you. Now does she?"

"I'm not Mickey!" Iggy Boy screamed as he covered his ears with his hands to shut out the sound of Jake's voice.

The minute Iggy Boy released his hold, Slater rushed to Casey.

Jake didn't let up. "That's right. You're not Mickey, are you? 'Cause Mickey wouldn't do these terrible things. Mickey wouldn't hurt a soul. Would he?"

"That's right, Jake. Mickey wouldn't hurt a soul." Iggy Boy fought for composure. "Wasn't that the problem?"

"Mickey was never the problem." Jake stood firm.

"Don't make me retch. Who was going to protect him, Jake? *You?*"

Iggy Boy's words evoked more pain in Jake than even Iggy Boy knew. "No," Jake answered sadly. "I didn't protect him."

"That's right, Jake. You didn't." Iggy Boy shook his head in disgust. "You couldn't even protect yourself. Iggy Boy had to take care of everything."

"For Mickey."

"That's right, Jake. For Mickey."

"Don't make *me* retch." Jake saw the look on Iggy Boy's face, the look that told him he was moving in the right direction. "You didn't take care of Mickey. You took care of yourself. Mickey didn't want that pretty little girl. Barely even knew her. And Mickey didn't want to hurt Sammy. Sammy was one of the only boys in that house that ever offered Mickey a kind word." Jake shook his head in disgust. "Iggy Boy." He spat at Iggy Boy's feet. "You ignorant, ignoble, ignominious, little worm."

For the first time, Iggy Boy looked frightened.

"Mr. Spegman would be so very proud of you, boy," Jake continued. "It's just a shame they all wasted that name on Mickey, a shame they didn't know who *really* deserved it."

Iggy Boy lunged for Jake. He grabbed Jake by the throat.

"Jake!" Slater screamed as he rushed to try and help him.

"Not now, Sammy," Jake pushed Slater aside. "How many times I got to tell you I can take care of myself." Jake didn't even try to fight back. He just stood there, staring into those eyes as the hands tightened around his neck. "Listen to me, Mickey. I know you can hear me."

"Stop it!" The grip got tighter.

"I know some terrible things happened to you. Terrible things. Some terrible things happened to old Jake, too. And for the longest time, old Jake was hurtin' so bad that the only thing he thought he could do was run away and hide, just like you did, Mickey. Only old Jake didn't crawl way down inside himself like you did. No, old Jake hid away by trying to drown himself in all the booze."

The eyes that were staring back at Jake were now tormented and pained. And the grip around Jake's throat loosened a bit.

"But it don't work, Mickey," Jake continued. "It just don't work. 'Cause all you're doin' is hurtin' yourself more. And you don't deserve to be hurt no more, Mickey. You understand me? You don't deserve none of the hurt you've been carryin' around all this time. Neither one of us do." Jake saw the tears starting to well up. And the eyes that were looking back at him were now familiar. "Somehow, you've gotta stop this, Mickey. Somehow, you've gotta listen to your own voice. 'Cause old Jake knows it's in there. It may be buried underneath all the pain, but I know it's still in there. You've just gotta find a way to hear it, Mickey. And if you can't listen to your own voice just yet, you listen to mine. Find the strength you need in mine. 'Cause there ain't no crime in that, Mickey. Ain't no crime in *that* at all." Jake's own eyes started to well up. "Even old Jake had to listen to someone else's voice before he could recognize his own."

The hands around Jake's neck let go.

And for the first time in what seemed like forever, Jake saw Mickey.

"I hurt so bad, Jake." It was the only thing Mickey managed to say as the tears rolled down his face.

Jake held Mickey in his arms like a father comforting a child. "I know you do, Mickey. I know you do. But it don't always have to be this way. I promise you that. We're gonna get you some help, okay? We're gonna find a way to make this better for you." Jake looked to Slater and Casey. "Sammy," the name slipped out of his mouth before he could stop it. "You got a quarter on you?"

Slater nodded.

"Why don't the two of you go find the phone. Understand?"

"Sure, Jake." Slater took Casey by the hand and headed toward the hallway.

And as Jake cradled Mickey in his arms, the same way his granddaddy had cradled him when he was full of hurt and full of confusion, he couldn't help thinking about just how lucky he was to have had someone in his life who loved him so much—even if it was for such a short little while. "You hang onto yourself, Mickey. You hear me?" Jake couldn't hold back his own tears. "'Cause you're a good boy, Mickey. A real good boy. And no matter where it goes from here, you just remember that."

CHAPTER · 40

Casey headed toward Bowdin House with the letter in her hand. She hadn't opened it. The return address and the size of the letter told her everything she needed to know.

Out in front of Bowdin House, Jake was mulching the flower beds. He got to his feet as Casey approached. "Well, hello there, Sunshine," Jake smiled. And before she could even answer, from behind his back he produced a spectacular bouquet of spring flowers. "Old Jake had a feeling that congratulations would be in order." He nodded toward the envelope in her hand. It was her acceptance to Brown.

"How did you know?" She smiled. It was almost a rhetorical question. By now, Casey was aware that Jake knew everything that went on at Huntington Prep. And everyone else was waking up to that fact, too. No one ever referred to him as Flakey Jake anymore.

"I knew because you're not the only one who got

one of those letters today. There's somebody inside that house who's picking up his mail right about now. And my guess is that any minute he's gonna be runnin' out that door to go lookin' for you. Ain't he gonna be surprised?"

Casey knew that Jake was right. So she decided to just stay where she was and wait for Slater to come out. "Thank you for the flowers, Jake. They're beautiful." In a way, it seemed a crime to cut them. Jake tended the beds with such love and care. And each one of them produced an explosion of color from early spring right through late fall.

"The only thing more beautiful than those flowers is your smile."

Casey blushed.

"And I guess you've got plenty to smile about today," Jake went on. "Couple of weeks, and you'll be leavin' here. And next thing you know, you'll be off to college, startin' a brand-new life."

"I'll miss you, Jake," Casey said sincerely. Jake had been like her guardian angel, always keeping an eye on her. She would miss that security. "You know I'll come back and visit you whenever I can."

"Not here, you won't." Jake had news of his own.

"You're leaving?"

"Retiring," Jake told her.

Just then, Slater dashed out the door of Bowdin House and down the front steps, just as Jake had predicted. Jake and Casey shared a knowing grin.

As Slater headed toward them, Casey held up her letter for Slater to see it. He laughed in delight and held up his own. They were going to Brown. Together. Slater was following family tradition. And Casey was following her dreams. They hoped they could somehow manage to keep pursuing their goals together.

"Slater, Jake's retiring!" Casey shared the news.

"You are?"

"Figured it was about time for me to be movin' on, too," Jake explained. "And, thanks to your family, I'll be doin' it in style."

"My family?" Slater looked confused.

"Yessir. All these years I've been livin' here at this school, I've never had to pay rent or worry about my meals. I haven't had any expenses to speak of, and nothin' much else to be spendin' my pay on. So I've been savin' my money, investin' it. That's where your family comes in. The way I figure it, the Laurence family is smart. And good people, too. So whatever they do with their money is probably a good idea. Whenever I read about some new business that your family was gettin' into, I'd put some money in, too. You'd be surprised how it adds up. Fifty dollars here, a hundred dollars there. Yeah, over twenty years, it sure does add up. Old Jake's got a real comfortable life to look forward to."

"That's wonderful, Jake." Slater patted him on the arm. "Nobody deserves it more than you."

"Where are you going to go?" Casey wanted to know.

"Florida," Jake announced happily. "The Sunshine State." And all three of them laughed. "Bought myself a condo down there. And I want the two of you to come and visit me. Florida's not just for old people, you know. It's a fine place for young people, too."

"You bet we will," Slater assured him.

"Absolutely," Casey confirmed it.

"You know what," Slater said. "I think all this good news deserves a celebration. Why don't the three of us go out tonight for a pizza? How 'bout it, Jake?"

"I think that's a great idea. Anything the two of you want. And it's on me."

"No way," Slater said. "I don't care how rich you are, I did the inviting, so I'll do the paying."

Jake laughed. "You're a good boy, Slater Laurence. A real good boy." He patted Slater on the back the way he always did. "Okay, then. We'll go out for pizza tonight. On you," he conceded. "And afterward we'll go out for some ice cream. On me. But before that, I got plenty of work to get done around here."

Jake headed off to another one of the flower beds,

leaving Slater just standing there, mouth agape. "I can't believe it," he said finally, shaking his head. "Did you hear what he said?"

"Yeah." Casey was equally stunned, and certainly amused.

"He called me Slater Laurence. Can you believe that?"

"No, I can't." Casey had to stop herself from laughing. "Why do you suppose he would do that . . . Sammy?"

His blue eyes sparkled and Slater laughed, wrapping his arms around her. He pulled her close and kissed her.

♠ ♠ ♠

Jake saw them, out of the corner of his eye. And he smiled. Because he couldn't help feeling like he was a little bit responsible for their happiness. And as he watched those two beautiful young people walk off with their arms around each other, he heard his granddaddy's voice whispering in his ear.

"You're a good boy, Jake. A real good boy."

About the Author

A.G. Cascone is the pseudonym of two authors. Between them, they have to their credit three previous books, two horror movie screenplays, and several pop songs, including one top-ten hit. This is their first novel of horror and suspense.

**A mesmerizing new trilogy
by Wolff Ryp**

MIDNIGHT
Secrets

"You will know me as Revell," he told her.

At first Kendra thought the handsome
stranger who haunted her dreams existed
only in her imagination. Now she knows
Revell is as real as flesh and blood. He is
utterly irresistible—and totally evil. For
centuries he has preyed on young women,
drawing them to him—then killing them.
Unless she can stop him, Kendra will be
next.

The Temptation
0-8167-3542-5 $3.50
November 1994

The Thrill
0-8167-3543-3 $3.50
December 1994

The Fury
0-8167-3544-1 $3.50
January 1995

Available wherever you buy books.

And don't miss . . .

TOWER of EVIL

by Mary Main

A horrifying secret hides within its walls

Since the terrible fire that destroyed her home and took her parents, Tory's only family is the aunt she's come to live with on the California coast. Lonely and grieving, she finds herself drawn to a strange neighbor and his silent, reclusive daughter. Tory senses that Dag and Elissa are hiding something, but even she is unprepared for the dark secret she uncovers about them. It defies everything Tory has ever believed, yet its terror is all too real. Now Tory's own life is in danger. Can she survive the Tower of Evil?

0-8167-3533-6 • $2.95